The Trial of
CONNOR
PADGET

a lawyer's gamble

AF123838

The Trial of
CONNOR PADGET

a lawyer's gamble

CARL ROBERTS

Where Authors are Family
Columbus, Ohio

This book is a work of fiction. The names, characters and events in this book are the products of the author's imagination or are used fictitiously. Any similarity to real persons living or dead is coincidental and not intended by the author.

The Trial of Connor Padget

Published by Gatekeeper Press
2167 Stringtown Rd, Suite 109
Columbus, OH 43123-2989
www.GatekeeperPress.com

Copyright © 2019 by Carl Roberts
All rights reserved. Neither this book, nor any parts within it may be sold or reproduced in any form or by any electronic or mechanical means, including information storage and retrieval systems without permission in writing from the author. The only exception is by a reviewer, who may quote short excerpts in a review.

ISBN (paperback): 9781642374834
eISBN: 9781642374841

Library of Congress Number: 2019930476

Dedicated to Patrick

1

It was after five o'clock, and I was sitting at the bar of the Gunga Din waiting for Connor Padget. The Gunga Din was changed, no longer the bar it had once been, not since the sailors from the merchant ships anchored nearby on the Mississippi River had discovered it. Most were Hispanic but there were Germans too, and a few whose native tongue was Dutch. Gradually the use of English words and phrases disappeared. The stockbrokers and accountants, once loyal customers, departed—went north three blocks to the Hofbrau House with its half-liter steins of beer and a female accordion player.

The owner was a realist. He muted the television and bought a wall clock depicting the U.S. Marines raising the American flag on Iwo Jima.

Connor was not at the bar when I arrived. I didn't worry, but now the clock showed five twenty, and I wondered. On the television Channel Nine was switching from news to sports. The sports announcer had barely smiled his good evening when an orange banner flashed across the screen. Channel Nine was announcing breaking news. The portraits of two African

American jazz musicians hung in the background, which meant the news crew was in the lobby of the Baton Rouge Airport. In front of the portraits stood Joe Reed, WAFB's roving reporter.

Reed was top-notch, a man of composure, respected for his level-headedness and, with a nose for tragedy, a man who covered every calamity within helicopter range of the city. He began to rehearse, leaning into his unique on-camera slouch, head tucked in close to the microphone.

Suddenly he pulled up and began to trot. As he picked up speed, the picture zoomed in and out of focus, but he never broke stride. He trotted past the airport's Gourmet Corner, past Dunkin Donuts and Wendy's. It was when he passed the Bass Pro Shop that I spotted Connor in his purple LSU windbreaker and ball hat.

On the screen three men emerged from the tunnel for arriving passengers. Faces straight ahead and somber, all three ignored the commotion surrounding WAFB's stakeout. The man in the middle was handcuffed. He was dressed in a denim jacket and fancy cowboy boots. The two men on either side of him wore light sport coats and dark slacks. The three of them moved steadily toward the camera and were approaching the Bass Pro Shop when Connor stepped forward, raised a pistol, and fired. The man in the middle slumped. Connor dropped the gun and lifted both arms in surrender.

My mind began to tumble. Connor and I had played on the same basketball team at University High, had worked at the Dairy Queen during the summers, had gone off to LSU together. He dated Mary Beth, his high school sweetheart. When she became pregnant, he left LSU, married, and started work at the post office.

Not more than a week before, he'd confided in me, right here at the Gunga Din. He was concerned about Mary Beth. He thought she might be cheating on him. He paid little attention to the Monday night game. Wasn't the game our reason for being here? He sat and fidgeted. I didn't want to believe what I was hearing, but he might be onto something.

"I got more proof on Thursday," he said.

Being a lawyer and thus no psychiatrist, I had a dislike for suspicions without evidence. It could simply be his own paranoia. I could but watch for signs.

"You want to tell me?"

I didn't really want to know. It was easy to accept the abstract notion that husbands and wives go amok, but I didn't want to hear about a Mary Beth gone wild. She and I were friends from high school, and I liked her.

"I'm not going for a divorce. I don't want to risk losing custody of Scot."

"Sounds reasonable."

He began tracing a circle with his finger on the bar. His finger slowed, then began a steady tapping. "No offense, Jack, but I don't trust judges, and I don't like lawyers."

I wasn't offended. I too disliked divorce. In my opinion lawyers often just made things worse for a couple already under stress. I answered, "You're still at home then."

"I moved Friday... I'm at the Bon Amis apartments now. I'm going to wait this guy out. Simple as that."

"At least you have a plan."

"Scot's started taking karate lessons," Connor continued. "That's how all this began. Last Thursday I found out Mary Beth's taking lessons too. She was keeping it a secret. Why? I'll tell you why. She's getting her karate lessons for free. How do I know? The lessons are a hundred twenty-five a month per person. I checked last month's bill. It was exactly one twenty-five."

His facts were stacking up. Still I was reluctant to believe Mary Beth had gone off the rails. "Who pays?"

"You know Mrs. Dameron's dress shop on North Boulevard?" he asked.

"I do."

"Mary Beth works there now. She says she's tired of being poor. That's how she pays for Scot's lessons." He shrugged. "She blames me. And guess what, I blame me too."

"She simply wants a paycheck to help pay a few bills. The Mary Beth I know is like that."

His finger tapping sped up. "She said we're second-class citizens."

"That's harsh." It was easy to find fault. Day by day husbands and wives accumulate grievances. My wife, by now, had accumulated points against me and I against her. What were we to do with our stored-up points? Could Adrienne even remember now why she had once fancied me? I had no answer.

Connor straightened on his stool and looked at me. "Like I said, I'm going to wait this guy out. That's my plan. I think it'll work. This Alfred Pohl—that's his name. He's a wanderer. Soon enough he'll get tired of Baton Rouge and move on."

"Sounds good to me," I said.

Several days later, I was standing on the fourteenth green of the Wandering Creek golf course when I spotted Connor jogging up the cart path. Something must be up. I walked over to meet him and waited.

He stopped to catch his breath. He was upset. "Adrienne told me where you were. Sorry to interrupt, but I want you to get an injunction. I need it right away. Could you file something Monday or Tuesday?"

I stalled, trying to figure out what to do, and turned back to my playing partner. "Be with you in a minute, Phil." A few days ago Connor hadn't been interested in filing for a divorce. Now he wanted an injunction. It didn't make sense. I shook my head. "You can't just go around asking for injunctions, Connor. You have to file for a divorce first. What's got you so upset?"

"Scot's going to Memphis with Pohl. Some damned tournament. I want that stopped."

I reached out, touched his shoulder. "I'm sorry, Connor. A judge wouldn't want to involve himself in this."

He shrugged and my hand fell away. He didn't answer. Just stared at me.

"I wish I could be more optimistic. But the law can't solve everyone's problems."

"If anything happens..." He gazed blankly at the cart path. "If anything happens up in Memphis, who do I hold responsible? You tell me that, Jack."

"I don't expect anything bad will come of this. Why should it?"

"The karate instructor isn't taking any other boy. Only Scot. You don't have kids, Jack. You don't get it. I know something's wrong here." He turned away, walked back down the cart path and headed for the parking lot.

That had been a week ago. Connor had come to me distraught and in search of help. Now he would stand trial for attempted murder. I glanced at the wall clock. It read five twenty-six. I paid for my drink and left.

2

I stood in the foyer of our home, listening to the sounds of Adrienne running up the stairs. I had called to her loud enough to be heard, but there was no answer. Was she avoiding me?

I made my way to the freezer and the chilled bottle of Stolichnaya and was struck by the oddness of this business of living. Seated in the breakfast room nook, I could drift back in time, have my Russian vodka, and recall, as if it were yesterday, the time I'd spent in Japan flying covert missions over Russia. On our spy flights Wayne Sloan and I had searched and tracked the Russian radar sites on Sakhalin Island. There were nights when we flew unmolested, nights when we were too good for them to find us. Even those nights that they found us, we broke loose from the MiGs, put the plane into a dive, skimming the waves and flying hard until we were safely home. Then came the night one of the MiG's missiles struck home and sent us crashing into the Sea of Okhotsk. In the morning when the helicopters came for us, I was alive, my arms wrapped around Sloan's dead body.

I heard the sound of Adrienne's footsteps on the stairs. I looked toward the doorway and waited. "Oh, there you are,

Jack. I didn't know you were home." I admired Adrienne and had always been happy at the first sighting of her. What I was unsure about was her reason for lying. I felt certain she'd heard me come in.

"Sorry to be late. Connor got into some serious trouble tonight." She frowned. I continued, "He shot someone. At the airport, live on the five o'clock news. I saw him do it."

"Is the man dead?"

"I'm not sure, but I don't think so. I'm going to the jail in the morning to see him."

"Good Lord."

"I'm going to represent him."

"You're not a criminal lawyer, Jack."

"I'm a trial lawyer, Adrienne. I'm good in a courtroom."

"Have you considered what Mr. Fuller will say? Firms like yours don't touch criminal cases."

"Fuller might understand. Connor's a friend, not a client."

She raised her eyebrows. "Don't do it, Jack. Fuller will never allow it. You're putting your career in jeopardy. You know that." She turned to leave and gave one of her kindly smiles to let me know she was being patient. "I left your dinner in the oven." She wasn't through with me yet. She arched her back. "You've upset me with this Connor business. He's a friend from high school, Jack. It's a tragedy, yes, but it's not your fault. You should not get involved in this. I'm going upstairs. Don't think for a minute I'll change my mind."

Watching her stride off, I understood two things: she was concerned that I would represent Connor and her mind was made up about building in Beau Arbre.

Her idea for this house had begun last Thanksgiving with the arrival of an invitation from Sessions Sinclair to view the antebellum Beau Arbre plantation. I didn't doubt the old plantation property would sell. Sessions had a reputation for having the keenest eye in the city when it came to real estate. No doubt any number of grand homes would be built in Beau Arbre and gracious people would live there, but living there would put me in a funk. I preferred a simple life.

I left the breakfast room and made my way to the small alcove at the rear of the house where I would spend the night. This sanctuary of mine had come about by accident, a result of Adrienne's not wanting to hang a photograph of my spy plane in the den. She'd never been able to understand that when I lived in Japan, that plane was my home. In compromise she'd hit upon the idea of the alcove, an out-of-the-way room I could call my own. I looked at the RB-57 photograph, hanging there as if in midair. For three years now, she'd kept her promise never to intrude.

I was possibly headed for trouble in the morning with Fuller Bright & Swayze, but for now I was content to sit in my old leather chair with a glass of Stolichnaya and watch *The Tonight Show* from New York.

3

The attorney-client room in the parish jail was depressing with its worn couch, chipped table, and dented folding chairs. It was a shabby room with the smell of failure. I waited for Connor, wondering if anything good could come from such a place.

I heard footsteps and looked up to see Deputy Trahan. Connor was standing beside him, a sober look on his face. Trahan slid the steel bars to one side, and Connor walked in. He pulled out one of the chairs, sat down, then looked at me. "I didn't make it to the Gunga Din, did I?"

I felt a touch of anger. "What in hell came over you? What did you think you were doing?"

He began tapping his hands together. "You're my friend, Jack. But you're not part of this."

I'd gone off on the wrong foot. What I had said was born out of worry, not intended as a reprimand. A lawyer was forced to deal with facts, and the fact was Connor was in deep trouble and couldn't admit it. I would have to be more careful. I tried again. "Why don't you tell me what happened?"

He looked at his hands. "Pohl was like a curse. He appeared out of nowhere like some specter. Why my family?"

"Who knows. Some call it fate, some say it's karma, some blame it on coincidence. Hell, we can't even agree on a name for it."

He lifted his head and looked straight at me. "I'd shoot the bastard again. I'd shoot any man who kidnapped my son."

"I checked with the hospital this morning. There've been complications, but at least he's not dead."

Connor frowned. "I don't care. Maybe you think I should, but I don't."

"Scot was a spunky kid to escape like he did. How is he?"

Connor's eyes brightened. "He's with Mary Beth. With time he'll be okay, but he's had a bad scare."

"I heard the Memphis police brought him back on one of their planes."

"They were terrific, Jack. Brought him straight home where we were waiting."

"And the next night I waited for you at the Gunga Din."

His face became serious. "He deserved it. He's a pedophile."

I chose my words carefully. "Do you know that?"

He shook his head. "Pohl was going to stand trial for kidnapping anyway, so the police decided it wiser not to bring up the subject so that at his trial, Scot wouldn't have to testify about sexual stuff."

"So, nobody really knows what happened."

"Mary Beth and I decided to leave it up to Scot to tell us when he was ready, and he hasn't said much. He's just glad to be back home."

"Sounds like a good way to deal with it. It's been a shock to everybody. I'm going to defend you, Connor. I want you to know that. I'm going to file a motion for bail and get you home again."

He looked away. "You're a high-priced lawyer, Jack. You make a lot of money, and your time is valuable. The court will appoint a lawyer for me. I'm okay with that."

"The judge will appoint me if I ask."

He shook his head. "I'd feel like a burden. I don't want to be a burden to you too."

I stood. "I think I can get you off. You were protecting your family. My job is to convince a jury to believe that. That's what lawyers do."

"Maybe."

"The court hears motions to set bail on Mondays. You'll be home Monday night."

"Thanks, Jack." He looked confused. "Thanks for coming. You're a good friend."

"No problem. Don't think too much about it. Jails have a way of getting into your head. I'm here to help you. Call me if you need anything, okay?"

I turned to leave and looked back. He was still sitting on the couch. Deputy Trahan looked up as I walked past him on my way out.

By the time I reached the sidewalk, I began to consider the question of insanity and how best to measure it. In some ways, I didn't believe Connor to be any more unhinged than Fuller, senior partner of Fuller Bright & Swayze. I had become aware of Fuller's quirks early on, even though in these times, odd behavior often slipped by unnoticed. Spotting it came about in the most mundane way. Each day at twelve forty, partners of the firm gathered for lunch at the same table in the Hilton. Margaret, our waitress especially assigned to us, would appear smiling in her pink uniform. She was steady and reliable, as unchanging as the menu. She was also patient with Fuller.

Fuller as senior partner always maintained a firm hand on the tiller, and he took great care when issuing instructions. "I'll have a double Dewar's," he'd say, "with an unopened bottle of soda on the side." He would hold the menu, reading from it as if seeing it for the first time, though the Hilton on the River sailed a steady course. He would delay, as if waiting for a proper time to pass, then glance at Margaret. "I'll have the fresh garden salad with house dressing. I'll also have the roasted chicken with the creamy and crispy scalloped potatoes and carrots with spiced yogurt."

I couldn't say how long it had taken me to weary of his way of ordering. The menu offered but one choice of chicken, only one type of potatoes, and the only carrots available were topped with spicy yogurt. It was the same when he ordered trout or veal. He would never simply say, "I'll have the veal," or "I'll have the trout today." With his need to be precise, he would order precisely: "I'll have the veal Scaloppini with morel mushrooms" or "Today, I believe I'll try the blackened trout with spicy kale."

To my way of thinking, this was acting out of some kind. What possessed a person to behave as though he were speaking afresh when day after day he was ordering the same food, from the same waitress, in the same dining room of the same Hilton on the River hotel? There was but one answer: Fuller was an obsessive-compulsive, a man bent on controlling everyone around him and a dangerous man to work for.

4

A crisis was brewing at Fuller Bright & Swayze. It was seven thirty in the evening. I was at my desk dictating a legal brief for an emergency hearing before the Louisiana Supreme Court on Saturday. Exxon was under serious environmental attack, and the law firm of Bowling, Bennet, and Kean had failed them. At eight thirty-nine this morning the Exxon Board of Directors had contacted Calvin Fuller to save them. Mr. Fuller was good at such things: emergencies where there was little time for hours of research, where the attorney must already know the jurisprudence. Fuller was just the right man for such a job. He had graduated from Yale Law School with honors, been President of the Louisiana Bar Association twice, personally knew the justices of the Louisiana Supreme Court, and, most importantly, was gifted with a photographic memory. Earlier in the day I'd spent an hour with him, taking notes, and making a list of the appellate cases he deemed critical to the position we should take. With the meeting ended, I was left to my own wits and reasoning to produce a compelling brief as he termed it.

My phone rang. It was my secretary, Becky Tessier, who, out of loyalty and the promise of tomorrow off, had agreed to stay with me through the evening.

"Your wife is on line one, Mr. Carney."

Normally Adrienne didn't call the office. She was good about that.

"Hi, Adrienne."

"I'm calling to make sure you didn't forget."

I didn't answer, simply waited for her to tell me exactly what I had forgotten. I'd thought of little else besides Exxon since my meeting with Fuller, for he had made it clear that I should consider Exxon's problems as my problem. Since then I'd pushed everything aside, even hunger. I'd settled for a ham and cheese on toast brought to me by Becky.

"The architect will be here at eight," she said. "Do you know what time it is?"

Normally I left the office no later than seven and reached home by seven thirty. "I'll be lucky to be home by midnight, Adrienne. I have an emergency brief for the supreme court to finish. It has to be in the mail by midnight." I took a breath and held it. Bad luck had turned into good fortune. I hadn't liked Fuller dumping this Exxon problem on me, but now my working late had its advantages.

"You're happy, aren't you, Jack? I can hear it in your voice."

She was dead right. I was pleased with not having to deal with this Thomas Piggott of hers, and yet I didn't want to upset her. "There's nothing I can do about it, Adrienne. I apologize."

"Well, I'm not at all happy, Jack." I heard a click.

Not bothering to knock, Fuller walked in. He never knocked. When he saw I was on the phone, he grimaced, his eyes narrowing in disapproval. "The brief must be postmarked by midnight. Will it be?"

"I have it under control."

"Then I'll leave." He turned and left as abruptly as he'd appeared. The anxiety Fuller brought into the office lingered, and I glanced at my watch again. Exxon was a serious enterprise, and I was engaged in important work. I began to dictate. Connor's problems and Adrienne's would have to wait. Left alone I should finish and be able to deliver my work to Becky by ten thirty. She and I would be gone from the office by eleven fifteen.

At eleven thirty I headed out, reached the sidewalk and decided to walk the five blocks to the post office. A walk in the night air would do me a world of good, allow me to clear my mind of Connor as well as Fuller. My thoughts turned to Atticus Finch, a small-town lawyer who possessed the gift of discernment. I'd learned of Atticus from Professor Pugh, a teacher of contract law at LSU. He did not socialize with students, tolerated no nonsense, and was a favorite of almost all. In a way, he was frightening.

On the first day of class he introduced himself. "I am Denson Pugh. My purpose is to instruct you as to the law of contracts. Some of you are bright enough to be attorneys, others of you are not. Perhaps those of you who are not are more suited to become piccolo players. The world in my view is more in need of piccolo players than lawyers. My task is to separate the lawyers from the piccolo players."

Professor Pugh paused, removed his glasses, and spoke in an earnest tone. "My hope is that among those of you who become attorneys, one or two of you will see the practice of your profession as Atticus Finch saw it. As for those of you who've never heard of Atticus, I suggest you learn of him."

CARL ROBERTS

I had reached the steps to the post office and my thoughts of Atticus drifted away; in the real world I worked for Fuller Bright & Swayze and had business to attend to.

5

"Did you have a nice golf game, Jack?" Adrienne eyed me with a half-smile.

"Hopkins played well. I made a mess of a couple of holes."

"We should have Hopkins over sometime. Would you like that?"

She was trying to be nice. That was good news. "I wasn't aware you thought much of Phil." Normally Adrienne would not have seen profit in socializing with someone like Phil, a man in his fifties without the proper sort of ambition, a man satisfied with being in charge of the pro shop at a place like Wandering Creek Golf Club.

"I was simply being thoughtful." She patted her hair, usually a sign she was nervous. "It's true I don't think highly of where you choose to play. It just has that little concrete building. It seems so desolate."

We didn't see eye to eye concerning Wandering Creek. It had been carved from a hundred and forty acres of pine trees with a creek running through it which nourished the wildlife that lived there. More than once, at twilight, I had watched deer run and frolic along its fairways. "It's a golf course," I said, "a place set aside only for golf. I like that."

"It doesn't compare to the Racquet Club. We both like the Racquet Club."

"That's true."

The Wandering Creek Club was not on level terms with the Racquet Club where a member could shop for tennis clothes, choose the best in suntan lotions, even purchase a diamond-studded tennis bracelet. Upstairs the club hosted wine tasting seminars and formal dances. In addition, the restaurant was unique, the only place where a person could order the famous Racquet Club salad.

Unlike the tennis pro, Phil Hopkins was not a maker of money. He was a man who had failed on the PGA tour and gradually came to know who he was: a man who loved golf and could scrape by with running a golf shop. The way I saw it, Hopkins and Wandering Creek were a good fit for they had each come up a bit short.

"Hopkins kidded me about your being wealthy."

"Hopkins kidded *you*...about *me* being wealthy?"

"I said it was your money."

She was quick. She stood pirouetting, then tugged at her shorts. "And I intend to spend it." Stopping her pirouette, she shimmied her hips. "It's providence, Jack. God wanted me to have money. No one dreamed dad's duck blind was sitting on a huge pool of oil. He didn't know it either. It's my inheritance, Jack. It just dropped down from nowhere...and I'm thrilled to have it. You should be too."

If she had remained the girl I married, we might have succeeded in making a life together. Now I wondered if that were possible. I glanced away, took to gazing at the mimosa trees growing beside our brick cooking pit. I smelled the mimosa scent of nutmeg and decided it would be wrong to argue. She was going to build her West Indies style house in Beau Arbre; it was a problem with no answer.

"Aren't you happy here, Adrienne? I am."

"Yes, of course. It's a wonderful house." She patted her hair again. "I saw Susan Spencer at the Racquet Club."

"And?"

"She and Stu are building in Beau Arbre. We'll be neighbors."

The scent of nutmeg evaporated, replaced by the sour smell of mud three thousand feet below the Atchafalaya Basin. I could hear the sound: the whumping and clanging of the Exxon Mobil drilling rig, raising up money which neither of us had need of.

"Are you sure this Thomas Piggott's a good choice? I heard there's something peculiar about his eyes, that when one eye looks straight at you the other doesn't. Dick Barton, at the firm, thought that might be a problem."

"Oh, Dick Barton. He exaggerates everything. Thomas is highly respected. He's built some of the finest homes in the city."

I didn't wish to pursue the matter. After all, none of us was without a blemish or two. Still, I had no use for a British styled West Indies house and thus no use for Piggott.

She leaned near. "If you don't meet, I'll just deal with him on my own." She almost smiled. "So, you might as well meet him. And I guarantee you will."

"We'll see." I looked Adrienne over and realized what I liked most about the Racquet Club. She was a fine-figured woman, and it thrilled me to see her in tennis clothes.

She looked at me in her coy way. "I don't think a five-thousand-square-foot house is pretentious, do you?"

"It'll cost about two hundred dollars a square foot."

"Oh Jack, I can afford that. Besides, we can live there forever."

I poured a vodka and tonic and drank it halfway. "I'll no doubt be miserable. You'll be so happy at first, you won't notice. Then one day you will. Soon you'll think I'm being ungrateful."

She slid one leg over the other, and I looked at her thighs. "We'll live in separate houses and commute for sex." With an impish look, she popped from her chair, undoing two buttons of her blouse as she spoke. "Fix me a vodka, will you?"

I reached for her glass, ignoring her peach laced bra as best I could. She undid the third button.

6

At exactly eight fifteen I opened the door of Fuller Bright & Swayze. "Morning, Becky."

"Morning, Mr. Carney. You have calls."

She handed me slips of pink paper. She was tall, almost statuesque, had a neat feminine way of writing, and I liked her. She seemed to like me too, and we worked well together, but that only counted for so much. Once I was safely out of sight, she would buzz Ms. Forman, who would make a note that I'd arrived fifteen minutes late. The note would be written in the firm's demerit book, which Fuller reviewed at the close of each week.

Looking out the window of my office toward the Mississippi, I felt safely tucked away. The view had been a reward for successfully defending the lawsuit by Victor Delahoussaye's estate against General Dynamic and Gulfstream. Delahoussaye had flown his Gulfstream G550 into the ground a mile short of the runway at the Louisiana Regional Airport. The lawsuit had been a cause of some concern, for Delahoussaye was a prominent oil man from Lafayette with wealth enough to own his personal Gulfstream and with heirs who would receive a great sum of money for his death if they could pin the accident on the Gulfstream.

After a week in the courtroom, I had persuaded the jury that Delahoussaye had killed himself: that it was he who had decided to fly into a heavy thunderstorm, that it was he who, with lightning flashing about, had lost his nerve and flown his plane into the ground.

This case made me recall my years in the Far East. Winters in Japan were dreary; there were weeks when the weather hung so low it hugged the earth. Those were the days the weather could kill you as easily as the Russians. That was how I remembered one night at Yokota AFB.

Our mission had gone well, and we were in the landing pattern, coming in on final with the weather so thick it obscured the runway. We were passing through seven hundred feet when the voice of the ground controller crumbled. Suddenly we were listening to his coming apart, heard the pain in his voice as he sobbed, "Fuck it. Fuck it. Oh, Fuck it!"

Immediately we climbed, trying for altitude, trying to save ourselves, all the while listening to his screaming. We flew, waiting for a new controller to replace the airman who had broken, waiting for a new airman who would speak to us, quietly guide us, not into a rice paddy but onto Yokota's runway. Who had saved us that night? Who had allowed the air controller to fall apart, preventing him from bluffing his way through and killing us? Had it been the unseen God? I didn't know, but I thanked him for it.

I would forever love Japan and the men I flew with. Sometimes I would think of them and wonder what they would make of the path I was traveling with a man like Fuller. I remained at the window, waiting for the rain to obscure the river. Not until all trace of the river had been blotted out did I sort through my messages.

Eloise Vetter, court reporter and videographer, had called to remind me of the deposition in the Childress case, which was scheduled for nine thirty. The file was somewhere on my desk, and, as I located it, my phone buzzed. I counted the buzzes. If it buzzed more than three times, it would mean Fuller was attempting to lay hands on me. What Fuller did not know was I was on the lookout for him. This morning I had my own business to tend to. In a few moments, irritated that I had not answered, he would set out to track me down. The wisest course to take would be to leave immediately or risk being caught up in whatever he had thought up for me.

Tossing my raincoat over my shoulder, I headed out, made it to Miss Tessier's desk. "Becky, I'm leaving for deposition in the Childress case. Wish me luck."

She gave me a sly look as if she knew I was up to something. "Mr. Fuller's looking for you. And your deposition isn't till nine thirty."

"I need to leave early because of the rain."

"He knows you haven't left. I told him so."

Fuller's office was back down the hallway, and I headed that way. The door to his corner office was closed, for it was the custom of this law firm that each attorney work hidden away. I slipped on my raincoat to present myself as someone who had business to tend to. Opening the door, I saw him bent at the waist, dictating away. He glanced up.

"Have a seat, Jack." He continued dictating, "… all of which is most respectively submitted to this Honorable Court … I see Miss Tessier tracked you down."

"I was just leaving. Deposition in the Childress case."

"We need stamps from the post office. I've asked Ms. Forman to draw a check."

Having partners run errands at a firm like Fuller Bright & Swayze was certainly a disrespect of our positions. While it somehow seemed to satisfy Fuller's need to make sure we knew he was the final word as to firm policy, we lesser partners thought the oddity gave us a type of freedom, freedom to get outside and see faces on the sidewalk and talk to postal clerks about mundane things. But today I was irritated he had turned my secretary into his watchdog.

I shook my head. "I have to be at Vetter's. I have a deposition at nine thirty. Besides, it's raining."

Fuller was not easily deflected. "Okay, okay. Go by the post office after the deposition."

"Yes, sir, I can do that." I was satisfied with the new arrangement. I'd gotten away with saying no, had forced him to reach an accommodation with me as if I were a person. I decided to push my luck.

"Sir, did you watch the local news last night?"

He fidgeted, glancing around his desk as though looking for something. "No, waste of time mostly. Why?"

"A friend of mine was involved in a shooting at the airport. A camera crew was there."

His head jerked. "You say this fellow is a friend?"

"Yessir, he is. Connor Padget."

Fuller was no fool. "And you propose to represent him?"

"With your permission."

"Am I to understand the shooting was seen on television?"

"WAFB."

Fuller shrugged. "Why drag the firm into it? Surely he'll be convicted."

"I'm not so sure. He shot a man who kidnapped his son, perhaps molested him. The jury will be sympathetic."

I thought I saw his face twitch as he stared at me. "I don't consider the practice of criminal law appropriate for this firm. But then, of course, he's your friend." He looked away, reached for a file and opened it. "I'll think it over. Try to be on time for lunch."

He was finished with me, ready to move on, so I left as quickly as I could and headed out into the rain. With the soft leather stamp bag tucked under my arm, I headed for Spanish Town. The Spanish settled here first, but in time they'd been replaced by the French, as happened in New Orleans. Eventually the French disappeared as well. Small law firms had taken over, turned the cottage-like houses into places of business. The old brick sidewalks were uneven, pushed this way and that by the roots of trees that lined them. With its small-town, neighborly atmosphere, I thought it a fine place to practice law.

At the corner of Fuqua and Napoleon, I caught sight of the small frame house with soft grey shutters, the offices of Vetter Court Reporters & Videographers. Inside the reception room, Jerry Campbell was waiting with his client. Her husband had lost control of his car on the old four-lane highway between Baton Rouge and New Orleans. The accident had claimed the life of her husband and their twelve-year-old daughter. The wife suffered serious injuries and so had her nine-year-old son, who sat beside her on the couch.

"Excuse me if I'm late," I said. "I decided to walk."

Jerry stood. "You're not late, Jack. It's only nine twenty-five." He turned towards his client. "I'd like to introduce my client, Mary Evelyn Williams, and her son, Lee."

Mrs. Williams rose from the couch, smiling and wishing to appear friendly. She extended her hand as if to shake mine, then let it drop. I didn't wonder at her reluctance. No doubt she viewed me with distrust, someone who stood between her and the money she would need now that her husband was gone. It wasn't a matter of trust. I had no grudge or grievance with her. I was but someone in possession of a file containing the opinions of experts who, having examined the wreckage of the family Ford, gone over it with their fine-toothed comb, had not uncovered a single engineering defect. If there was a need for further proof, I had that as well. My file also contained a report from a reputable accident reconstruction expert that Mr. Williams had been traveling at least eighty-five miles an hour when he lost control.

Later, when the deposition was over, I left on foot, avoiding puddles of water left by the rain, which had moved on. Mrs. Williams had not given in to her tears during my questioning of her, for she had been steadfast in saying she'd kept an eye on the speedometer and her husband's speed never exceeded sixty-five miles per hour. The tears didn't come until I showed the reports of the experts to her attorney and she saw his reaction. He thanked me and said the truth, "This case will never come to trial."

This lawsuit of hers was a desperate act, an attempt to seek redress where no redress was due. She had been an eyewitness to his reckless driving, sat beside him as he endangered their lives. She had known from the beginning that the automobile had played no part in their family tragedy. As for me, I had done what I was paid to do. I should feel no regret, and yet I did. What great wrong had she done? If she'd spoken up, demanded her husband drive with more care, would he have responded? Who could answer such questions? I was certain of but one thing: I was growing weary of skirmishing with attorneys over money. And what of mighty Ford

Motors? Corporate executives were paid handsomely, could not a penny or two have been found for the widow?

Long ago a justice of the Supreme Court, a wise and considerate man, had written "Hard cases make bad law," and I knew he was right. Once an attorney begins to doubt such an axiom, he is no longer much use to himself and is a danger to good order. Perhaps it was time I set sail for Florida. Once there I could open a simple bait shop where the only news worth hearing would be whether or not the fish were biting.

7

I had seen to Connor and set a date for his bail hearing before the court. For me this was a free day. Now I was on my own with no one to answer to. I left directly from my home on Terrace, driving my Mustang onto Interstate 12, heading east toward the strawberry capital of the world. Sixty miles away lay Hammond and, though I'd been this way before, I had always driven past it on my way to the beaches of the Mississippi Gulf Coast. Today I had business in Hammond. Tucked safely in my briefcase was a check for five hundred seventy-five thousand dollars made payable to Judah Baine, attorney-at-law, and his client Bobby Tricou.

Tricou, a young man in his twenties, had lost his right leg in a barge accident on nearby Lake Maurepas, and Judah and I had settled on the value of Tricou's leg. Three months had passed since I'd taken Tricou's deposition for the purpose of gauging what sort of witness he would be in front of a jury. Bobby and I sat across a table with a court reporter, transcribing our words and a video camera taping. He was a well-built young man with a friendly manner who answered questions simply and directly without a hint of drama. He was the sort jurors would take to, for they were bound to see him for what he was: a man who was prepared to take on the misfortunes of life without complaining.

I exited the interstate and parked in front of Judah's office, a remodeled carriage house across from the Amtrak station. A prim grey-haired secretary greeted me, led me along a hall to Baine's office. He was on the phone, standing beside a large leather chair. I liked the way he did business, for he was clearly a gentlemanly lawyer who did not keep people waiting.

I took a seat. His mahogany desk was carefully kept, neatly polished and wiped clean. What puzzled me was why a human skull sat upon it.

Finished with his conversation, he extended his hand. "That was Victor Politz, President of First Community Bank. He'll be ready for us in twenty minutes." He paused, swept the room with a wave of his arm. "This is your first visit. So, tell me what you think."

"I like it."

"Do you like the print over the fireplace?"

I glanced toward the mantle and the painting of David and Goliath. "It's beautifully done."

"Late sixteenth century, Caravaggio."

"It's quite nice."

He shifted in his chair and gestured toward the skull. "That's real you know."

"Interesting. But why?"

His face lit up. "It was common in the Middle Ages for monks to keep a skull on their desks while they worked. I think it keeps life in perspective, don't you?" He reached for his phone. "I don't want you going back empty-handed, Jack." He turned away to speak into the phone. "This is Judah. I have a friend here from the city. I'd like him to go home with some fruit. Thanks, three quarts will be plenty. We should be at the Community Bank in twenty minutes, so you can deliver them there." He turned. "That was CCP Wholesale. They sell berries to restaurants from New York to Chicago. Fly them out every day." He stood. "Back to business. If we leave now, we'll have time to walk."

As we turned right onto the sidewalk, he gripped my arm lightly. "It'll be a bit of a show at the bank. I hope you won't mind, but there's no harm in doing things with a flourish, is there?"

The bank president was waiting for us. "Welcome to First Community, Mr. Carney. Any friend of Judah's is a good man."

I looked about. Clearly, I was meeting someone who did not care for chrome or glass but preferred the look and feel of wood. Four teller stations were marked by wooden arches and dark wire mesh. The floor of the lobby had been laid not with cold marble but with stained pine.

The banker turned his attention to Judah. "We have everything in place. We're ready to roll."

Judah leaned toward me. "You should consider opening an account with Victor. He keeps a person's affairs private."

Victor smiled. "Here we don't worry much about Washington D.C. and, us being a community bank, they don't pay much attention to us. Works out. We do pretty much as we please."

I liked the idea of people doing pretty much as they pleased. To my way of looking at things, Politz was simply a man who wanted to run his own store. Didn't every level-headed person value their independence?

Victor stirred. "Let's get started, shall we? I'll lead the way."

I followed Judah and Victor past the tellers, taking note of the small glass jars filled with lollipops beside each of their stations. We turned into a large room with two security guards, armed and standing beside a table. Behind the table, Bobby Tricou smiled from his wheelchair. On the table was the largest amount of cash I'd ever seen. Near the bank's open vault stood a lady with a video camera filming away.

So, this was what Judah was up to. The joy and happiness of great wealth preserved on videotape. No doubt I would be shown handing the settlement check to Judah, who in turn would transfer it to Victor. The camera would pan to a closeup of Bobby and the money as if the check had been turned into cash. Once the camera was off, the cash would be returned to the vault, and an account for Bobby would be opened at First Community. Later Judah would provide a commemorative DVD, which Bobby would play a great many times for his friends and family. This Judah Baine from the small town of Hammond was more than a good lawyer. He was a fisherman who had learned how to cast a large net.

Thirty minutes later I was heading east on I-12. It was still my free day, and I had no intention of returning to the office. I would ponder my encounter with the free-spirited Judah over a lunch of softshell crab and draft beer at Middendorf's off exit 15. The story of Middendorf's had just begun. He and his wife had come to the waters of Bayou Manchac to seek a new way of doing things. They had built a grand place to eat with a view of South Louisiana's swamp and cypress trees. I could find no better place to mull over the ways of Judah Baine.

The softshell crabs, battered lightly and fried, were a treat and the beer icy cold. On impulse, I checked for messages on my cellphone. Kathy Postlewait had called. She and I had become friends when she followed a lawsuit resulting from an explosion at the Mobile-Exxon refinery. Eleven workers had lost their lives and the trial had lasted three weeks. I'd come to see her as a Rene Zellweger, full of pluck, ever on the lookout for good will in people.

On the fourth ring, she answered. "Glad you called back, Jack. I have bad news."

"What's up?"

"Alfred Pohl died at six thirty-five this morning from complications. The district attorney is charging Connor with first degree murder. I spoke to one of the nurses. She says the doctors were careless. Pohl died from septic shock."

I too was in shock. "I appreciate your calling, Kathy. Thanks."

"Wait, don't hang up. You have to be upset, but I'm a reporter. Do you have any comment?"

The waitress was coming toward me with the coffee and pie I'd been looking forward to but no longer wanted. "What do you expect me to say?"

"I want to know if you still intend to represent Connor?"

"Give me a couple of days. I'll let you know."

I looked out onto the large swamp cypress trees. They loomed like sentinels over the part of the world that had been given to them. The sun was on its way down, playing its part in the eternal passing of time. Soon, it would pause for a moment then plunge and disappear. Today Bobby Tricou had become wealthy but at a terrible cost, and I'd played a part in it. But the day had not been as kind to Connor and me, and both of us would have to deal with it.

8

From the basement of the courthouse I rode the restricted elevator that opened onto the jail. Behind the green wire-mesh screen of the duty officer's station stood Deputy Trahan. "What brings you, Counselor?"

"I came to see Connor. How's he holding up?"

Trahan reached for the gooseneck microphone. "Bring out Connor Padget." He turned back to me. "He's adjusting. You can wait in the attorney-client room."

The room was just down the hall. The lock clicked as I neared the door, and I went in to begin my wait for Connor. The next sound was the harsh clang of steel as the jail doors slid open, and there stood Connor in his orange jumpsuit. The escort deputy beside him seemed friendly but merely turned and left.

"You look fine, Connor," I said.

Connor hesitated, then slumped into the chair across the table. "Pohl's dead. A deputy told me. I guess that means I'm going to stand trial for murder."

"I'm afraid so."

He stared past me. "Remember that day on the golf course? I told you I had a bad feeling about Scot going to Memphis. I was right."

"I simply couldn't help. I'm sorry about that."

"What happened to Pohl? I was told he was in stable condition. People were saying he would make it."

"I can't say for sure, but the rumors are the doctors were negligent. A reporter for the newspaper told me, but she also said no one could ever prove it."

His face brightened. "Then I didn't really kill him. It was the doctors. That's right, isn't it?"

"I wish it were, Connor, but it isn't. The law doesn't see it that way. The law says because you shot him, you were the proximate cause of his death. It would be the same if the ambulance taking Pohl to the hospital had gotten in a wreck and he died from that. The law says you're the guilty one because it was you who set things in motion."

"That doesn't seem fair."

"I can mention it at the trial. It'll get you some sympathy. You're going to need a lot of that."

He straightened in his chair, looked directly at me. "He was an intruder, Jack. Like some parachutist dropped from the sky to ruin my life. The world is a better place with him gone."

I wanted to say how sorry I was. Instead I said, "Stay with me here, Connor. It's natural for you to be emotional, but that doesn't help. We need to build a plan."

He stared past me. "The other inmates say what I did was right. They say they would've done the same. Anyone who loves his children would agree."

"Inmates don't sit on juries. The jurors are the people we have to concentrate on."

He shifted in his chair.

I reached into the pocket of my jacket, laid a photograph on the table. "This man went by the name of Lavrentiy Beria. He was in charge of the Soviet secret police under Stalin. His job was to get rid of Stalin's enemies. He told Stalin, 'Show me the man and I'll find you the crime.' He became famous for that."

"My crime isn't very hard to find. I shot the guy in full view of TV cameras. I don't get it."

"I'm not talking about you. It's Pohl I'm after. A man who would kidnap a child has a past. This wasn't his first crime. I went looking on the Internet—searching for a starting place— he was arrested for counterfeiting in Arizona."

"You mean he spent time in jail?"

"No. The charge was dismissed. Police misconduct."

He leaned back in his chair. "That proves my point, Jack. Sometimes people need to take the law into their own hands. He wouldn't have been able to kidnap Scot if he'd been in jail where he belonged. You have to admit I'm right."

"What-ifs are not facts. The jury wants facts, not what might have been. I think he left Phoenix because he was probably being watched. I'm filing a Freedom of Information request with the FBI. That's bound to turn up more dirt."

"Can you do that? Just find out everything about someone's life?"

"Not as long as a person's alive. But dead men aren't protected. Privacy's no longer an issue once we're gone."

"I don't want to be skeptical, Jack. But I'm afraid I may be done for."

"There's not much else I can do, Connor. I can't play detective and search out the real killer like you see on TV. I mean… you're the one who killed him."

He looked down at his hands, started rotating his thumbs. Then he looked up again. "You could be right—he was a predator—you're bound to find something."

I reached for a pen and the small notebook in my jacket. "It's my understanding the deputies brought Scot to your house the day before the shooting."

"That's right. It was late in the afternoon."

"Did either of you ask him if he'd been molested?"

"He was so happy to be home. We didn't ask...thought it better to wait."

"Let's talk about the shooting. How did you know when Pohl would arrive at the airport?"

"The deputies told me. I asked them what was going to happen to Pohl. They said they were bringing him back the next day to stand trial for kidnapping. I asked how they were bringing him, on the sheriff's plane or a commercial flight. They said on the sheriff's plane, scheduled to arrive at five."

"So you knew when he was coming in. When did you decide to meet the plane?"

He leaned back in his chair. "I was at work. Nothing was normal. Everybody said how they hoped Scot would be all right. It got to me, like I needed to do something. I went and got my gun." He paused. "Even when I was driving to the airport, I'm not sure I meant to go through with it. Then I saw the snazzy cowboy boots he was wearing and the stuck-up look on his face—that's when I shot him." His voice broke. "He was a no-good, Jack. A shit."

"That's a hard story, Connor. It's important too. It shows you're not a criminal. You're no threat to society. You were trying to defend your family."

"Be straight with me—can you get me off?"

"We have to see what I find. I can't say more than that right now."

"I'm worried about Scot. I want to see him. Is he all right?"

I shook my head. "Not yet. It wouldn't be good for him. Too many things in flux. It'll be better when things settle down."

"I appreciate you standing by me, Jack. But I'm not sorry I did it."

I looked around. "How's the routine here?"

"About what you'd expect. I'm trying not to let it get to me. It would help if I had some books."

"You used to like Robert Service."

He smiled. "*The Cremation of Sam McGee.* I always loved that."

I laughed. "It would be a gruesome tale if he hadn't written it with so much humor."

"Yeah, cremating his friend inside that old relic ship…he had to make that seem reasonable, and he did." Connor reached for the photograph of Beria and slid it across the table to me. "Let's hope this Russian was right."

I stood, stuck the photograph back in my briefcase and knocked to let the deputy know I was ready to leave. "Don't worry… the Russian was always right."

9

The following morning at eight fifteen I stood at my desk looking at *The Morning Advocate*. I had little doubt it was the work of Fuller. *The Advocate* had printed a photograph of Connor shooting Pohl with the headline, "Airport Shooting Turns Deadly." Pohl's dying had caused things to take a turn for the worse, and I feared there was more to come. Sitting in my chair, trying to think things through, I spotted, tucked neatly into a corner flap of my desk calendar, Fuller's note.

> We'll discuss your continued representation of Mr. Padget at today's firm luncheon. Regards, Calvin Fuller.

I didn't doubt this was a cause for concern, but the firm luncheon was still four hours away, and for now I had other fish to fry. I was dismayed how Connor viewed the trouble he had brought upon himself. He was still speaking as a person incapable of seeing the wrong he had done. He said he was sorry it all happened, but it was as if he were confessing to having gone for groceries and come home with a box of Frosted Flakes rather than Raisin Bran. How a jury would react to such a lack of contrition was painful to contemplate. And what of the decision makers at *The Advocate*? My hunch was they would see Connor as a vigilante and launch a crusade to demonize him. They would dig deep into his background for missteps, search out neighbors and co-workers for gossip. Readers of the newspaper would become curious and any mention of Connor would become gold for the selling of papers.

Scandal and notoriety were headed Connor's way, but some good could be gotten from it: readers would pay good money to see Connor's name in print, and my plan was to provide *The Advocate* with a way to do just that. Crusades, like fires, are in need of constant nourishment, and I intended to do business with *The Advocate* if I could.

The reception desk at *The Advocate* was a curved table decorated by woven straw baskets filled with silk flowers. Behind the desk sat a woman eyeing me as if she knew I was in need of help. "May I be of service this morning?"

"I'm a partner with Fuller Bright & Swayze. My name is Jack Carney. I'd like to speak with your Director for Community Affairs."

She reached for the phone. "That would be Ms. Bettison. I'll ring her."

Soon a nice-looking woman with auburn hair came toward me. "I know Owen Swayze quite well. I'd be happy to assist you."

"I came to open a charitable fund. I hoped *The Advocate* would inform its readers."

"But of course. Please come this way." She set off down a corridor, and I followed, wondering if her friendship with

Swayze was something that should worry me. Seated in her office chair, she reached for pen and paper. "Let's begin with a few details, shall we?"

"I'm naming it the Connor Defense Fund."

She reacted, blinked, and carefully returned her pen to the desk. "Is this the Padget involved in the airport shooting?"

"Now that Mr. Pohl is dead, I'm afraid Connor will be charged with murder. I'm a friend, and he doesn't have a great deal of money."

She straightened, stiffened in her chair. "If you don't mind me speaking freely…" She waited politely. "I find it quite out of the ordinary for a firm like yours to involve themselves in a criminal case. I must ask…does your firm know about this?" She didn't continue, simply gazed at me. I was not offended; she was right to ask.

"The firm will have no connection with Connor or the fund. I'm representing him on an ad hoc basis."

She relaxed. I pushed on. "I believe the trial will generate a great deal of interest. *The Advocate* could benefit by taking part. After all, it was your competitor, WAFB, who was at the airport."

She brightened. "You have a point. *The Advocate* owns WBRZ, and they weren't there. Too many people see Connor as a WAFB story." She reached for her pen. "What if *The Advocate* created a daily box score to track incoming contributions? We could outline the box in dark ink and run it daily on the front page below the fold. Perhaps…" She stiffened as if the adventure of creating something had passed. "*The Advocate* will require complete access to all accounting of receipts and expenditures. All fees paid to you will, of course, be closely monitored."

"I won't be charging a fee."

She gave me a skeptical look. "Why won't you? The people in this city are generous. There should be enough for attorney fees."

"Let's be realistic. Connor will be convicted and spend time in prison. The question is for how long. This money is for his family."

She stood and extended her hand. "I believe we have an agreement, Mr. Carney. A final decision will be made by the managing editor and the legal department. I should be able to get back to you within a day or two. I must say this has been an interesting morning."

Back in the hallway I noticed a woman standing at the water cooler, her green skirt pulled taut around her buttocks. As I drew near, she turned. "My Lord, it's Jack Carney."

"Morning, Kathy." I was happy to see her and grateful she had called with the news of Pohl's death.

"I've been trying to call you. Your office didn't know where you were."

"I've just come from seeing Ms. Bettison. I'm opening the Connor Defense Fund. What do you think?"

"Good idea." Her eyes twinkled. "I have good news. Adam Boatner wants to interview Connor. Is that okay with you?"

Boatner was the anchor of WBRZ's early morning broadcast. He was likable and had a reputation for respecting his guests. Yet I was doubtful. I thought it probably not a good idea to let Connor speak for himself. "Let me think about it, Kathy. Don't want too much publicity at once."

"Well, what about you? I could get you on the *Midday* show with Ann Doherty. She has good ratings, and her audience is loyal to her."

Kathy was good at her job, and I was fortunate to have such a friend. "I'll do it." Good things were coming my way. This was a moment to store up in my memory for when hard times came, as they surely would.

***

Owen Swayze, a man of habits, had always taken a seat beside Fuller at the firm luncheon. Today he chose the seat next to me. Could it be Ms. Bettison had spoken to him about my visit with her? I studied Fuller for a sign of something on the horizon. He was acting normally at the moment, sipping his Dewar's. Not until the scotch was half gone did he change.

He removed the swizzle stick from his glass and carefully laid it on a napkin. "I have a fundamental question to put before the firm." He paused, glanced first at Swayze, then at me. "The question is a serious one as it affects the reputation of us all. Should the firm accept a client charged in a grave criminal matter which will generate a great deal of unwanted publicity? Personally, I am opposed to abandoning our long-held tradition of limiting our practice to civil matters."

The question, along with the answer, had been neatly put, and no partner would oppose Fuller. Sharp pain struck, and my stomach knotted. I was in a predicament brought on by my own doings. These partners were all decent men, honorable attorneys who practiced law and supported families. If Connor was a burden, it was mine alone.

I still had a way out. I could recant, abandon Connor. These men would forgive and forget, take my behavior as an aberration, a momentary slippage in judgment to be swept under the rug. If I persisted, I would not be tolerated.

What was to be made of my way of thinking? What would a lawyer like Atticus Finch say to me? When all the water had been boiled out of the pot, what was left? The truth was that we, as attorneys who had succeeded, were persons of privilege. How many times had I listened to the lie that the litigation I was involved in was a matter of principle? The truth was and would always be that it was about money. What measure of money would equate to the sacrifice of the life of a Wayne Sloan? Looking about me, I was willing to admit that I liked these partners, but respecting them was a whole different problem.

Owen Swayze jumped in. "Clint Fraiser is the man for the job. He's the best criminal lawyer in the city. Connor might have a chance if he hired Clint."

Swayze's comment was like the closing of a door, for he had offered a viable alternative to my headstrong waywardness.

Fuller appeared happy as a lark. "I believe we have our answer. This firm will refer any possible criminal clients to Clint Fraiser."

I said, "Connor's not a criminal, Mr. Fuller."

"I disagree."

"You didn't grow up with him. You didn't go fishing with him on Old River or go possum hunting with him where we now have the Ogden shopping center. You don't know Connor. He's just a name to you, a name in the newspaper."

Fuller straightened his back. "I've always done what's best for this firm, Jack. It's our policy to stay out of criminal cases for a reason. You know that."

"I understand your concerns. But Connor can't afford Clint Fraiser. He's facing possible life imprisonment, and I can defend him. I can get him a much lighter sentence. He's not a murderer."

"Are you requesting a vote from the firm?"

All of us knew the firm would continue to do nicely without me. The firm was a creature with its own being and would function as usual. Not one, not two, not any among us were indispensable.

"I could ask for a temporary leave while I try the case. But that wouldn't eliminate the firm name being associated with criminal matters. We all know that. Still… I can't abandon Connor when it's possible I can save him."

Fuller looked from one partner to another. No one spoke. "Anyone in favor of Mr. Carney defending Connor Padget shall signify his vote by standing."

Mr. Swayze stood. "I admire your loyalty, Jack, but tradition and precedence are important in the legal world. I'm with Calvin."

Fuller was accustomed to victories. I could picture him at home this very evening, speaking of this incident to his wife, treating it as nothing more than firm gossip. The Sea of Okhotsk flashed across my mind. The night gave way to dawn and a small dot in the sky grew larger until I knew it was one of our helicopters looking for Sloan and me. Then, as suddenly as it had appeared, the scene vanished, and I was once again looking at Fuller.

I could no longer control my anger. I stood. "Please accept my resignation."

If the partners were taken aback, it could not be seen on their faces. Mr. Swayze spoke in a calm voice. "You've made your decision and we'll miss you, Jack. I'll instruct our accountants to send you a check for your share in the partnership."

"Right now, I don't give a damn."

Fuller picked up his fork to resume eating. What needed to be said had been said. Yet I was still standing. I placed my napkin on the table, turned away, and left The Hilton on the River.

10

Adrienne's Lexus was parked beneath the porte-cochère when I arrived home. For a moment I was content to admire our fine Georgian home, trying my best to overlook the fact that my wife believed it no longer suited her.

This searching of hers for a more acceptable lifestyle had begun innocently enough. We had taken to traveling to New Orleans for the day. We would roam the Garden District, breathing in the old-world charm of the homes, topping the day off with dinner at Commander's Palace.

Without my noticing, Adrienne's delight had turned into a fancy, sprouting into a mighty oak from the acorn of nostalgia. Overcome with a longing for the grandeur of days past, she'd finally settled on a picture-book British Colonial West Indies house. With her search at its end, she had become a willful Southern woman with the means to get what she wanted. She wanted to live happily for the rest of her days in a dream of her own construction.

As for me, I had grown to love my simple Georgian home, and I would not leave. I pushed open the front door to the foyer, surprising Adrienne, stopping her dead in her tracks.

"Jack...what on earth?"

"I startled you. Sorry."

She was wearing her hair down, letting it drift over her shoulders. I felt a pang, which was always how my yearning for her began. "I took the afternoon off."

She gave me a coy look. "I have news. I'm excited." She stretched out a leg, much as a dancer would do, and headed for the den. I watched her walk away, watched her hips moving and shifting. For the moment, I was happier than she would ever understand. Under the circumstances, my run-in with Fuller was news that could wait. I made for the kitchen where I found a bottle of Dubonnet and a bowl filled with ice. It was obvious Adrienne had been celebrating her good news already. I reached for a cocktail glass, poured a double shot of Russian vodka. I knew not why, though perhaps it was my disagreement with Fuller, but I began to remember the Russians who had done what they could to end my life.

We were on our way home. It was nearing sundown, and we thought we had made it safely past their search for us again. Suddenly a plane was on our radar, closing too fast to escape now, and I steeled myself for ejection. I held no grudge, had come to accept that the pilot who had ended Sloan's life and almost taken mine was but a man like us doing his job.

Leaving a remnant of vodka in the glass as was my custom, I poured in the Dubonnet, then went looking for Adrienne. She was lying on the couch, curled up against one end, her bare feet sticking out from her jeans.

"I brought the bottle," I said.

"Marcie called. She's starting a church and wants us to join."

"A church?" What could be made of such news? It was quixotic, not unlike Adrienne's wanting to live in the handsome fashion of the heyday of British colonials. Had some attraction for the odd come over the people I knew and liked? Marcie was a gregarious woman, neighborly and sweet, but not someone I had pictured as knowing much about the workings of God. Was she experiencing a feeling of uselessness? If so, I could identify. My Sanibel Island fantasy was similar. I would do a good job, sell my Texas rigged plastic worms at a fair price to people who loved fishing. Within the hour, the customer would have a string of bass and experience the pleasure of being alive.

Adrienne reached out her glass, and I poured in the Dubonnet. "It's going to be a real church. They've named it Amazing Grace Chapel."

Adrienne's news deserved mulling over. Marcie was a churchgoing Catholic, yet she was sailing into unchartered waters. I didn't doubt she had her reasons, for she was a lady of good judgment. Perhaps she was looking for adventure. If she was on the hunt for something new, she could do better. She could open a convenience store where her affability and business sense would shine. She could begin with a single Marcie Mart and, with hard work, give Stop-N-Go a run for their money. Soon her Marcie Marts would be doing business city-wide.

"Have they found a minister?"

She smiled with pride. "John Keats, and he has quite the story to tell."

"Which is?"

"He's from Beaver Dam, Wisconsin, and he spent his first year of college at the Naval Academy. You should appreciate that."

"I respect the military, that's true."

"He didn't return to the Academy for his second year. He felt a calling and backpacked for a year in India. He said he was searching for God."

"Any luck finding him?"

"Jack, don't be cynical. He did have a profound religious experience after his meeting with the Dalai Lama."

"What did he do next?"

"He traveled to Japan. You should like him for that."

"Japanese are Shinto, not Buddhist."

"Of course. Keats says once you walk through the door of peace, you learn from others."

"I hope he doesn't go around saying, 'Have a blessed day.'"

"Wait till you meet him, Jack. You'll like him."

I remembered the words on the wall of our squadron's briefing room:

> The mission you are about to fly is dangerous, but you have two chances.
>
> You will either be shot down or you will return.
>
> If you are shot down, you still have two chances;
>
> You can escape and evade or be captured.
>
> If you are captured, you will either escape or die in captivity.
>
> If you die in captivity, you still have two chances.

"Give him a fair chance," she said. "That's all I ask."

I shrugged. "I'll give him a fair chance. Do they have a building?"

"They were quite lucky. The old Episcopal church near the law school is now a restaurant. The owner is a Unitarian. He offered to sell the rectory next door. They now have a gentleman's agreement that the Unitarians can use the rectory every Sunday between two and five."

I smelled the sweet smell of Gnosticism and thought of the first day I was told everyone on our team was entitled to a trophy. "I'm for people getting along, but I don't like the notion of abandoning Rome."

"You don't even go to Mass anymore."

"I still consider myself Catholic."

"Marcie warned me you might hide behind Catholicism. She said it doesn't make her any less Catholic by going to Sunday services at Amazing Grace. After all there's only one God."

What purpose was there to begin one's own place of worship other than to proclaim you had come to see the unknowable God in a new light? "I'm not comfortable with the idea of people starting their own church. Did Marcie say anything else?"

"She said I should be nice to you." She rolled over on the couch, fixed her legs to face me. Could she be signaling me? It was a chance worth taking.

"Let Marcie know to expect us on Sunday."

She popped up, swinging her legs from the couch. "You can be sweet when you want to—and I do believe it's time for these jeans to go in the wash." With that said she dropped the jeans to the floor, kicked them across the room.

The news that Pohl was dead and that Connor would stand trial for murder would upset her. But such news could wait until breakfast in the morning. That I was no longer a member of Fuller Bright & Swayze would be even harder to accept. I would have a great deal of explaining to do.

11

At eleven fifty-five, I took a seat across from Ann Doherty on the set of *Midday in Louisiana*. A tall, willowy woman from Syracuse, New York, she'd graduated from Tulane and married a professor of zoology at LSU. Though I'd never spoken to her, I had seen her on stage at the Magnolia Little Theater. We sat quietly without speaking, counting down to air time.

A lady in jeans running the camera flashed a sign. Ann Doherty's eyes began to sparkle and she looked into the camera. "We have as our guest today Jack Carney, attorney for Connor Padget, who is charged with the murder of Alfred Pohl." She smiled briefly at me. "Thank you for being here today, Mr. Carney."

I didn't know Ann well enough to use her first name, but this was television not real life, and I intended to appear at ease with her for the benefit of the viewers. "Thank you for inviting me, Ann. It's a pleasure to be here with you."

She nodded in her friendly way. "Just so we're on the same page, Jack, I like to get straight to the point. At the

Baton Rouge airport, your client, Connor Padget, took a man's life. How does he feel about that?"

Having watched four hours of *Midday* tapes given to me by Kathy, I was on the lookout for questions about feelings. "All of us are saddened by the loss of human life, Ann. Connor is no exception."

"So, you're admitting Connor feels remorse?"

"I'll have to give you a yes-and-no answer on that. Yes, he wishes none of this had happened, but at the same time he feels as a husband and father, he was protecting his family."

"I have spoken with WBRZ's attorneys. They seem confident Connor will be convicted."

I was on good terms with the attorneys who represented WBRZ. They were all excellent attorneys and, like myself, had never seen the inside of a criminal courtroom. "It would not be proper for me to speculate."

"Even if the jury returns a lesser verdict such as manslaughter, Connor could spend some time in prison."

I nodded. "The maximum is forty years. Hopefully he'll get a much lighter sentence. He was defending his family. That's a right we all have, you know."

She leaned closer. "I see a great deal of irony here, Jack. Earlier you spoke of Connor acting to protect his family, and yet, because of his actions, he has left his son without a father and his wife without a husband."

I wondered if she was sincerely concerned about Mary Beth and Scot or was setting about to vilify Connor. Happily, for me it made no difference. She had opened a door.

"Ann, I share your concern for Connor's family. To that end, the Connor Defense Fund has been created. All money donated will help support Connor's wife and son. Kathy Postlewait of *The Morning Advocate* is overseeing the donations to ensure its integrity."

"Will your attorney fees be paid from this fund?"

"There will be no fees. Connor and I are old friends." I smiled as best I could. "I hope your viewers will donate generously."

She glanced at her notes. "Let's move on, shall we? I assume you're familiar with Lieutenant Trahan of the Sheriff's department."

"He's in charge of the parish jail."

"Lieutenant Trahan has provided me with background information concerning Connor. According to him, Connor suspected Pohl was having an affair with his wife and shot him in a jealous rage." She paused, lifted an eyebrow. "That's rather archaic wouldn't you say? Wives are no longer chattels of their husbands."

I couldn't disagree. Such behavior would reek of male chauvinism and would endear Connor to no one. "Connor was suspicious but had no proof that I'm aware of. Perhaps you should ask Mary Beth."

"I've already reached out and asked her to appear on *Midday*."

Mary Beth would never agree. She wasn't the sort. "People would certainly tune in to watch her."

Ann looked down at her papers. "Let's change perspective, shall we? Do you own a handgun?"

I owned two, but I saw no reason to disclose that. I also had no interest in irritating this lady who had given me the opportunity to speak about Connor. I smiled. "I'm a lawyer, Ann, so naturally I believe in the Constitution."

Her chin came up. "You're hiding behind the Second Amendment, Mr. Carney."

"The Second Amendment is part of our Constitution, and as an attorney I swore an oath to uphold that document."

A sly look crossed her face and her eyes twinkled. "So if the Second Amendment were replaced what would your position be?"

"The same—that I'm sworn to uphold the Constitution."

She squinted at me. "Mr. Carney, you're ducking my question. I'm asking for your personal opinion about handgun ownership. If your client had not owned a gun, he wouldn't have shot Alfred Pohl nor would he be in jail. Can you deny that?"

I smiled at her as if enjoying friendly byplay. "Lawyers are taught to stay away from what-ifs and stick to facts. But if you want to talk about Alfred Pohl, I'm happy to do that. Let's first take the fact he was a liar. But worse than that he was a child abuser. He kidnapped Scot. That's abuse. He preyed on the innocent. There's no telling what evil he had in mind. Connor tried to protect his family." I shifted my gaze from Ann to the camera lens. "He also made sure Pohl wouldn't be a threat to other children. It's unlikely Scot was the last child this evil man would have kidnapped."

"But your client took the law into his own hands. That's dangerous. You must admit that."

"There's no greater love than laying down one's life for another. I believe that, do you?"

"Yes, but—"

"My client was willing to offer up his life for his son. He was willing to be treated as a criminal, willing to spend the rest of his life in the penitentiary at Angola. Compare that, if you will, to Alfred Pohl, a kidnapper who is dead and gone—and society is a safer place for it."

"I don't believe in violence," she said, "but it seems that you do."

"I believe in the right to protect oneself and one's family. I also believe violence is a last resort."

She leaned toward me and pointed her pen at me. "Jack, I take you to be a lawyer with integrity, but that doesn't make you right. I, for one, agree with the district attorney, but I do believe Connor is fortunate to have you as a friend."

"Thank you for allowing me to represent Connor to your audience. I trust they'll come to see my point of view. Connor is no criminal."

She smiled and turned to gaze at the camera. "Once again, thank you for watching. This is, as always, Ann Doherty, and we try hard to bring the news to you in a special way."

When the red light on the camera went off, Ann stood and held out her hand. "Nicely done, Jack. That was, as we say in the business, good television."

"Thank you, Ann. You were more than fair, and I appreciate your allowing me to come on your show."

***

"Hey, Jack, wait up."

Mike Carmody bounded down the steps from the other hallway to WBRZ's office floor. He was a financial advisor with the soul of an engineer, happy to spend his day reading charts and graphs. He also was a man with a knack for helping friends. Because of his advice, I had purchased a modest mix of tech and consumer stocks that were growing in value.

Catching his breath, he poked me in the chest. "You're quite the celebrity, Jack. Saw you on *Midday* just now."

"Thanks. How's Maggie?"

"Busy as ever." He grinned. "I don't know how I'd do without her. How's Adrienne?"

I watched him closely to see how he would react. "She's worried because of my resigning from the firm."

He shuffled his feet and reached for my elbow. "I heard that. You must have your reasons."

"It's a problem. I might not have done the right thing."

We had played golf last April at the Sherwood Country Club, he as a member, I as his guest. Our pre-round steins of beer in hand, he'd taken me for a tour of the men's locker room. Carmody, newly elected chairman of the club, had set out to improve whatever he could. With his engineer's soul, he'd selected Brazilian walnut for the new lockers, explaining as we walked that this type of wood was recognized far and wide for its shine. On the first tee, he pointed to the new concrete cart paths, recently poured and glistening in the sun. What to make of such a friend? He was a good and honest stockbroker, a man widows could trust. What was wrong? Why did I prefer the men I had flown with, men who had offered their lives up in secret, men who would see no difference between a golf locker made of pine and one of Brazilian walnut?

Mike and I were playing well, enjoying the day. We were beginning the back nine, had hit our tee shots on number ten when he said, "I had lunch with Bob Parker. He's getting together a duck hunting trip to Pecan Island. You interested?"

"I am," I answered. I liked the idea of a duck hunt — getting together with men on a cold early morning over a breakfast of warm boudin and grits. After such a breakfast, we would fill our flasks with Jim Beam, then make our way to the pirogues.

These small boats were perfect to navigate the narrow channels to our blinds, where we would wait for dawn, when the mallards and teals began to fly.

"I'll count you in," he'd said.

We'd played on, Carmody shaking off the occasional poor shot, for he was an optimist at heart. As for my own play, I had fallen into a groove, and by the end of it had shot a score worth the bragging. When the bags were stored away, his in a Brazilian walnut locker and mine in the trunk of my car, we said our good-byes.

Today he was in a different mood. He patted me on the shoulder and spoke in a careful voice. "This trial. I guess you know what you're doing. But to my way of thinking—you're riding a tiger. Don't fall off."

I raised my eyebrows and forced a mock sideways smile. "It's a burden. Much more than I realized it would be. That's what I tell myself in the daytime. Then, in the middle of the night when I can't sleep, I tell myself, don't give up. Something will help break this case. It nearly always does. But he did kill a man."

Carmody looked away to answer. "Yes, Jack, he did."

12

Taking the district attorney's private elevator, I made my way into the hallway leading to his office. Benton Jones was careful with his time and would not have invited me to visit unless he had something up his sleeve. He was quick-witted, good in a courtroom, and had a reputation for winning. He had served in Vietnam with Special Forces, and as veterans, we had good reason to deal fairly with one another.

Last year at the local Bar Association party, we had found ourselves alone on the porch of a camp overlooking the Amite River. He fixed his eyes on the branches of a weeping willow tree which dipped into the rushing water. How many drinks he'd had, I didn't know, but he spoke without slurring his words. "This reminds me of Nam."

Perhaps it was the glint of the moonlight on the water which shone through the dark night. I didn't know. Whatever caused it, I knew the signs. Benton was traveling back, reliving what he could never forget.

I joined in. "When were you there?"

"The year we went into Cambodia. Same year we raided the POW camp at Son Tay. It was 1970. I usually don't talk about this shit." He turned to look at me, his eyes hardened with sadness. "I've heard you flew recon missions in the Far East. You guys had guts."

"We lost a quarter of our squadron to the Russians."

He placed his drink on the table and peered out onto the water. "The Russians were in Nam. Did you know that?"

"No, but I'm not surprised."

"When we raided the camp at Son Tay, we killed thirty-six of 'em. We counted bodies." He reached for his drink, lifted it as though toasting. "I took a Makarov pistol off a dead major. Have it sitting on my desk enclosed in Lucite. Drop by sometime. It'll lift your spirits."

I had never dropped by, never seen the Russian major's pistol, but now I would. I pushed the buzzer beside the electronic keypad and waited.

"Who is it?" Benton's voice.

"Jack."

"The code is 1970."

I punched in. Benton was sitting behind his desk, an unlit cigar clenched between his teeth. He used the cigar as a pointer, taking it from his mouth and gesturing with it towards a chair. Neither of us took notice of the Makarov pistol.

"Glad you came, Jack." He waited for me to sit across from him. "There's talk on the street you've quit Fuller."

"It's been coming for a while."

He rose and walked to the window overlooking the Old State Capitol. "What's your opinion of Mark Twain?"

"I've read most of what he wrote. Why?"

"He said the Old State Capitol was the ugliest sight on the river."

"Guess he didn't care much for medieval castles."

Benton moved from the window, took a bottle from a small refrigerator. "Would you like some water?"

I shook my head, listened as he continued. "There's an old ammunition shed beside the Capitol. Dates back to the Civil War. Each time I look at it I wonder about us Southerners. We are a churchgoing people with good manners. We respect our elders and are forever saying yes, ma'am and yes, sir. Explain how such people got themselves caught up in a war defending a vile institution. Makes no sense."

"Didn't someone say, 'Fair becomes foul and foul becomes fair'? I guess people get stubborn. Get blinded by their way of seeing, and then there's all hell to pay."

He cocked an eye. "Pretty much fits what your friend Connor did."

I agreed but saw no profit in saying so. "Connor did what he thought he had a right to do, a duty to do."

Benton tapped a pen on his desk. "Mark Twain said something else. He said never pick a fight with a man who buys ink by the barrel. Jack, if I asked you to stop talking to the media, what would your answer be?"

"I would say no."

He leaned back, placed both hands behind his head. "Murder is a breach of the public order. Is that how Ann Doherty looks at murder?"

Benton deserved an honest answer and I would give it. "She's television, Benton. Scandal has become entertainment. It makes for good ratings. She's a nice person, but she's television."

"Stay away from the media, Jack. They devalue the legal system. They treat us like performers."

Benton was right as I viewed it, but we were lawyers and saw things the way lawyers did. We saw courtrooms as sober places, not happenings to be packaged and sold as though a trial was a thrill ride at a theme park in Disney World. "I was out to raise money for Connor. That's all."

Benton eyed me sharply. "Television cheapens things. Stay off."

"As long as it helps Connor, I'll keep going on."

Benton reached for his laptop. "E-mails are pouring in. California, New York, hell I even got one from Nebraska. Here's one from Ann Arbor. Some students from the university calling themselves Students for Justice for Pohl."

I shook my head; the law was being taken out of the hands of the lawyers and thrown into the public square as vigilantism. And yet, if I were honest, I was taking part in it, stoking the fire. I shrugged, knowing I would not stop.

"I'll think about it. You have a point." I stood to leave. "Connor's not a murderer, Benton. We both know that."

I headed for my Mustang with thoughts of Kathy. It was three thirty on a Friday, probably too late to reach her at *The Advocate*. She'd once told me how much she looked forward to her weekends. I could try her by cell, but she wouldn't answer, and her mailbox would claim to be full. Only the managing editor at *The Advocate* had her alternate cell number.

I enjoyed being with her for she understood attorneys better than most. It was my fault for not having thought of her until I was leaving Benton's. Come Monday I could reach her at *The Advocate*. I would have lunch with her and discuss the Connor

Defense Fund and casually propose we take the Mustang for a spin along the back roads to the Mandeville Yacht Club. Once there I would show her the Yarnspinner. She would be a perfect sailing companion, and I'd be happy as a lark to have her aboard.

When we were beyond the jetties, I would release the genoa, watch her marvel as it popped and billowed. In no time we would be under full sail, nylon canvas rigged taut, two friends sailing in silence.

But that was in the future, no more than something to be hoped for. I would go visit the karate school instead. My hopes of going sailing with Kathy would have to wait.

13

Goodings strip mall was within easy reach on Government Street just off an exit ramp of Interstate 10. Jake's coin shop had been there for years and did a good business. A computer repair shop had recently rented a space and seemed to be doing well. This morning I was interested in neither. I'd come to speak to Gloria Doyle and her husband Fred, the people who owned and operated the Art of Karate Studio where Alfred Pohl had worked. The parking lot was crowded, but even on a Saturday there were spaces here and there.

I opened the door to the school and a buzzer sounded. The room was smaller than I'd expected. Black folding chairs were placed against the wall. A woman, her hair tied in a knot, came toward me. "I'm Gloria."

"I'm Connor Padget's attorney, Jack Carney."

Her smile disappeared. "Oh, it was all so terrible. It's just dreadful what happened to Scot. How is he?"

"He wasn't harmed physically, but of course his father's in jail, so things aren't over for him."

"I don't know what to say. What happened at the airport and all. It's so sad."

"I came to find out what you know about Pohl."

"I'm quite willing to be of whatever help I can. Perhaps we should talk in my office."

The office was neat. Several rows of photographs hung from the wall behind her desk. In the center was a photograph of a husky man crouched in a martial arts uniform.

"Take a seat." She turned toward a gray three-drawer file cabinet. "Pohl's file is right here." She laid it on her desk and thumbed through papers. "Mr. Pohl came to us from Phoenix, Arizona, with a letter of recommendation from Gibson's Martial Arts." She looked up. "They have a chain of studios in Arizona and California. Excellent reputation. We considered ourselves fortunate Mr. Pohl chose our studio."

"I wonder if the letter of recommendation is legitimate," I said.

She sat upright. "Why shouldn't it be?"

"Because Pohl was arrested for counterfeiting in Phoenix."

"Oh, no." She fell quiet.

"Why don't we call Gibson's and find out if they have a record of Pohl's having worked there?"

She hesitated, then handed me a sheet of paper. "Let's find out. This is Pohl's application. Gibson's number is listed there."

I dialed the number and waited. "This is Jack Carney. I'm an attorney calling from Baton Rouge, Louisiana. I would like to verify the employment of Alfred Pohl, P-O-H-L. Do your records reflect when he was hired and when he left your employ?"

It wasn't long before I had an answer. "I'm sorry, sir. No one named Pohl ever worked for Gibson's at the Phoenix school or anywhere else. Can I be of further assistance?"

"Would it be possible for you to fax an affidavit to me stating what you've told me? It would have to be sworn to before a notary and two witnesses and signed by the manager of Gibson's in Phoenix."

"What's this for?"

"Alfred Pohl was recently murdered in Baton Rouge. I'm trying to track his history. He submitted a job application to a karate school here in the city and claimed to have been employed at Gibson's."

"Gibson's certainly doesn't want its name connected with a criminal case. We'll be glad to get that affidavit to you. What's your fax number?"

Gloria was glowering. "So, Pohl was a liar."

"Indeed."

"I wonder what else he lied about?" she mumbled as though speaking to herself.

"What about the tournament in Memphis? Do you think there was such a tournament?"

She didn't hesitate. "Definitely, sponsored by MacMaster's World of Martial Arts. I have their announcement letter in my file, but I had no idea Pohl was taking Scot to Memphis."

"I'm beginning to get a feeling for what sort of crime Pohl was up to. Yes, we need to call the MacMaster's people."

She dialed the number. "Hello, this is Gloria Doyle with the Art of Karate school in Baton Rouge. I'm calling about the tournament you sponsored in Memphis. It was for students between the ages of ten and fifteen… yes, that's the one. Alfred Pohl, one of our instructors, brought a student of ours, Scot Padget, to the tournament. Do your records show they participated?" After a long wait she whispered, "No one by the name of Pohl was there.

She's searching for the boy's name." A moment passed before she looked up. "Scot's instructor was listed as Allen Parker."

She spoke into the phone again. "One more question. Your brochure stated that the last day of the tournament was Saturday. As I understand it, Scot's parents were told the tournament was extended through Sunday." She pursed her lips. "I see. The tournament concluded Saturday at seven… yes, there seems to be some confusion about the time the matches were over."

I interrupted, "Would you please ask for an affidavit that the boy was only there until seven on Saturday night and Allen Parker was listed as his instructor?"

She did so and hung up. "Mr. Carney, I want you to know we've made changes concerning out-of-town trips. None of our students can travel out of town with an instructor unless a parent goes with them. Also, my husband and I are planning to donate fifteen hundred dollars to the Connor Defense Fund. We're so sorry such a tragedy happened. We want to do our part in helping Scot's family as much as we can."

She picked up Pohl's file again. "Here's a note I made. It was after one of my conversations with him. He talked of having spent time in California. I asked him if he knew anyone in the movie business. He laughed and said of course, anyone who spends time in Los Angeles does."

"You've been very helpful, Gloria, and Connor's family will most certainly appreciate such a generous donation. They surely need it."

I asked her to make a copy of the invitation to the Memphis tournament and to let me have the original. "It's nicely done and will make an impression on the jurors."

She walked over to the copy machine. "We know very little about this Alfred Pohl. I wonder if we'll ever know who he really was."

I know one thing," I said. "When he traveled to Memphis, it wasn't for a tournament. He was up to something else."

14

I wanted to see if I was serious about sailing to Sanibel Island. I called Adrienne and left a message. "I realize it's short notice, but our foursome decided on a golfing trip to the Gulf Coast. We'll be staying at the Broadwater Beach."

I felt no guilt with such a lie. Instead, I felt free as a bird. When Adrienne called back she seemed relieved. After all, she was concerned. I was showing signs of stress. The only quid pro quo asked for and promised was that I return in time to take her to the chapel on Sunday.

With the Mustang top down, I enjoyed the wind and drove straight south-southeast to the Gulf. I popped in a George Strait CD — "Just give it away." This George Strait was onto something. His ode to a new beginning had turned platinum, a sign that a great many people shared my feelings. What is the worth of many things when a relationship's turned sour?

It was mid-afternoon and the traffic was light. I was making good time to the outskirts of Covington and no more than twenty minutes away from the yacht club. I slowed to the speed limit. Just ahead was a favorite spot of the Louisiana State

Troopers who were bent on writing their quota tickets for the month. They loved hiding among the crepe myrtles growing in a hollow in the median just past a curve. This same hollow was a marker for me, the place where you turned onto a side road to Charlie's Wharf Restaurant. Charlie's was just the sort of place that a girl like Kathy would know about, and I had plenty of time.

It was barely five o'clock, the early birds had gathered, and the room was crowded. I took a seat at the bar from which I had a clear view of Lake Pontchartrain. Many of the tables were occupied by small groups of women sitting in clusters of two or three, which I took as a good omen.

I sighted her near a corner window. Here were the two of us caught up in the fun of Charlie's raw oysters with the weekend barely underway and the Yarnspinner at dock just down the road. She and her two friends were laughing, forking up the raw oysters from their shells, dipping them into a rich red sauce and washing them down with cold beer. Girls such as these would have made plans, probably had reservations at a hotel with a swimming pool overlooking the Mississippi Sound and offering poolside daiquiris and margaritas. The three of them were no doubt bound together for the weekend and any attempt to separate one from the others was foolishness. Normally I would do nothing in the face of such odds, simply slip away unnoticed. But the tug of coincidence was strong. After all, I'd resigned myself to having lost her, and yet here she was.

I watched the three of them carefully. They kept at it, dipping their oysters into the sauce and ordering another pitcher of beer. There was nothing left but to act, to do the best one could and hope. I made my way through and around the crowded tables, taking the three of them by surprise.

"Hi, Kathy."

She looked at me and smiled. "Jack, how nice to see you."

"I called *The Advocate*. They said you'd just left."

"Is this anything to do with the trial?"

"It can wait." I did what I could to appear nonchalant. "I'm on my way to the yacht club in Mandeville."

Her eyes drifted to her friends. "We're on our way to Biloxi. This is Cynthia and Jackie Sue."

Cynthia and Jackie Sue smiled, happy to meet any friend of Kathy's, especially someone who knew the whereabouts of Charlie's Wharf Restaurant.

Kathy's eyes sparkled at the mention of the yacht club. "You never told me you had a boat."

"That's the reason I called. I was hoping to take you sailing tonight."

"A night sail sounds wonderful, but we've made plans. I'd love to go some other time."

Ah, sweet rejection delivered with a promise of yes in the future. I decided to press on. "I could have you in Biloxi and back with your friends by morning."

"I'm sorry, but no." She glanced at her friends and gave a tilt to her head. "We're staying at the Edgewater. Why don't you meet us by the pool in the morning?"

"I'd like that." Rejection turned to promise.

***

Anxious to reach the Yarnspinner and be on my way, I parked beside a pine away from the clubhouse. The soil, topped with sand and pine needles, was soft, and I made not a sound as I skirted the great room of the Mandeville Yacht Club. I made it as far as the rear corner before I was brought to a halt.

"Whoa there. Where're you off to?" Ted Scullen and Miles Favrot waved at me from atop the bannister railing. They were both partners at Harrison & Boyd, a New Orleans law firm, and normally I would have a drink with them and enjoy exchanging tales of law-practice absurdities and sailing stories. But not tonight.

"I'm on my way to Biloxi." Running into Kathy had changed things. Tonight, I looked forward to sailing off with a purpose, setting sail where, at journey's end, someone would be waiting.

"Come on up. Have a drink with us before you go."

"Next time."

They laughed. "Sounds like you're up to something, Jack."

They'd hit upon my secret, for I might very well be up to something. Even so I answered honestly. "Have to meet a friend at the Edgewater."

"Take care."

By five-thirty in the morning I was astern Cat Island, five miles from the beaches of Biloxi. The shoreline was visible, stretching out alongside Highway 98, outlined by the trail of vapor lights lining the highway. High above were the hotels with their elegant swimming pools, free suntan lotion, and resort-styled lounge chairs.

It wouldn't be long before I was there myself, chatting away with Kathy. I brought the Yarnspinner as close to shore as I dared without running her aground and dropped anchor.

Down below, I took my time shaving, heated up a can of corned beef hash for breakfast and began my wait. Nine o'clock was a proper time to go in search of Kathy. I had time for a swim in the cool brown water. There would also be time for a beer, then lying on the deck of the Yarnspinner, in the morning sun.

When the time was right, I stepped into the dinghy, began paddling through the gentle waves of the Mississippi Sound, and headed for the Edgewater Hotel. Crossing over the hard-packed sand and four lanes of Highway 98, I made my way up a knoll which ended in a grove of palm trees and banana plants. Searching among the guests beside the pool, I spied her lying face up, sunglasses covering her eyes. Something inside me leaped.

Out from my cover among the palm trees and banana plants I strode. "Morning, Kathy."

She lifted her glasses and gave me a smile. "Jack, you're here! Did you bring your boat?"

"You can see it from here." I pointed to the beach.

She stood, and the two of us looked out to see the Yarnspinner rising then falling away in the soft breaking surf.

"It's beautiful, Jack, but how did you get to shore?"

"I used my dinghy…"

She lifted her sunglasses and looked at me, half smiling. "You make it sound like an adventure. Is it?"

I gave her a shy look. "Then you'd like to go for a sail?"

"Let's have a drink by the pool first."

"Good idea. I need to stretch my legs…what do you wish to order, my lady?"

"A margarita, thanks." She was enjoying our morning.

I could now count two things we shared: courtrooms and the occasional margarita.

When I returned, she was lying flat on the chaise longue, her body taut in her mauve bikini. I handed her the margarita.

"Aren't we having a special morning?" she sat up and lifted her glass in a toast.

"Where are your friends?"

"They're having breakfast in bed. It's a tradition with us."

This was more good news. She'd skipped out on their ritual breakfast to spend her morning with me.

"Do you and your friends come to the Edgewater often?"

"Three or four times a year."

"I like Biloxi too. Our foursome comes here twice a year to play golf. It appears we have something in common."

"I'm a reporter. You're an attorney. There's a difference."

Was she seeking separation or teasing my clumsy flirtation? "Why did you become a journalist?"

She sat up to sip her drink. "For me, being a journalist was a way to become involved. A person should be interested in what's going on in the world. Don't you agree?"

"Makes sense to me. What of courtrooms? Do you like covering trials?"

"There's a thrill to it." She tapped at her glass. "Someone wins, someone loses. The uncertainty of it all. Now what about you? How did you end up in law school?"

"Odd things. Bits and pieces that came together." I had entered law school as an idealist and now viewed myself as a possible cynic. Would the same not happen to Kathy? She was a lady with spunk but being around attorneys could turn spunk hard. The day might come when skepticism hardened into cynicism and she no longer saw the importance of tight skirts and mauve bikinis.

"You speak of it as happenstance." She picked at a strap that had fallen off her shoulder. "I've got a secret to tell you if you promise not to repeat it."

"I promise. Not a word."

"James Fisher is retiring in a few months. I've been promised his job and his Sunday column."

"That's big. Congratulations!" This cast Kathy in a new light. Fisher covered the comings and goings at the State Capitol on a daily basis, was courted by committee chairmen, and topped it all off with a respected Sunday column. These legislators were powerful people who, in the twinkling of an eye, could pass laws that could make someone rich. It was obvious now that Kathy had an eye to the future. With her talent and pluck, it wouldn't be long until she left *The Advocate* and took a good job with *The Atlanta Constitution* where she would wait for a call from *The New York Times*.

I asked, "Where do men fit into your life?"

"I like men. I find them interesting." She lowered her sunglasses over her eyes. "We all value our independence, Jack. I've watched you in the courtroom. I know you. You guard it with your life. And you own a sailboat."

"Guilty." I held up my glass and grinned. She too cherished her independence, placed as high a value on it as I did. She would devote her life to running to-and-fro, chasing stories of worldly importance. On the other hand, I longed for a simpler way. Fishing the flats off Sanibel Island would be enough of the world for me. I was done puzzling over things such as this. People should be happy.

I stood. "I'll get our next drinks to go. We can take them with us aboard the Yarnspinner."

She reached for her bag.

15

As matters stood on this Sunday morning, I was content. The Yarnspinner was seaworthy, fit and ready to sail to Sanibel Island. Kathy and I, with a weekend between us, had become friends. And Adrienne, pleased I had kept my promise to come to the Chapel of Amazing Grace, was sitting beside me in a green silk dress, her thigh nudging mine.

John Keats stood before us at the lectern preparing to speak. These friends of mine who had patched together this place to worship were searching for God. So who was I, a fallen away Catholic, to think right or wrong of it?

My thoughts drifted. Adrienne shifted her hips, tilting her body, and whispered into my ear, "We're so lucky to have found John Keats, don't you agree?"

"Maybe."

Dressed in khaki pants and a sailor's blue turtleneck sweater, Keats appeared to be everything Adrienne had promised. With slightly tousled hair and soft eyes, he looked to be an agreeable sort. He might well be the kind of man who had discovered peace in Asia. When he began to speak, I was taken in at once.

"Be not afraid, for I have not come to judge the world but to save it." His voice was clear and strong as he welcomed us. He fell silent, his eyes studying us. "Are we to believe these words of Jesus? If the answer is no, what are we to believe?"

Once again he went silent, waiting for the tension to grow, then in a soft, barely audible voice he said, "There is a neighbor to your left and a neighbor to your right. Do you love them? They each make mistakes. They have faults. What does it matter? If you wish to find peace, you must love them."

He held up two books, one in each hand. "My left hand holds a book entitled *The Imitation of Christ*. My right hand holds a book entitled *What the Buddha Taught*. Which book is better, you ask? I say don't ask that question. I say count your blessings that two such holy men were given the gift of peace which they chose to share."

Far across the room, I saw a hand being raised. I leaned forward, got a clear view of Ken Barrow, an assistant professor of history at LSU. Keats had spotted him as well. "Yes, Ken, do you have a question?"

"John, I know your background. I came today thinking you would prefer the way of the Buddha. India has a history of preferring peace to war. Not so with Western civilization. As for Christ, he died in violence, and the Buddha did not."

Keats didn't take long to respond. "I believe wisdom teaches we should search for areas where we agree rather than for where we disagree. Convergence, not divergence, is what is important. Otherwise we will never become one. Don't you agree?"

"Yes, of course. But isn't it true that Western ways began with Cain and Abel? There's no similar story in the East."

"Everyone aspires to peace," Keats said. "Men and women who live in the West or come from the East are the same. If the West has fallen short, perhaps it's because we don't see each other as equals. After all, we do love our Super Bowls and World Series."

Ken shook his head. "Peace is hard work."

Keats smiled. "We all know the Chinese saying that a journey of a thousand miles begins with the first step, but it's true, isn't it? Let me say this: I believe the first step in learning to love is learning to forgive. The Buddha taught forgiveness. Christ forgave from the cross. We can learn from them."

Two rows away an older woman arose. "I don't want to argue, but Christ said he didn't come to bring peace. He said he came with a sword to separate mother from son, sister from brother. People who preach from high on a mountaintop can afford to preach peace and joy. Not so with those of us who live in a world mixed with sorrow."

"No doubt you've suffered misfortune to speak in such a way. I pray that you put aside any resentment and discover peace." Keats might well be a man who preached from high on a mountain, but he was also a man who knew how to maintain control. With the room quiet once again he continued.

> Lord, make me an instrument of your peace:
>
> Where there is hatred, let me sow love;
>
> Where there is injury, pardon
>
> Where there is doubt, faith
>
> Where there is despair, hope

> Where there is darkness, light
>
> Where there is sadness, joy

"Hallelujah!" a loud voice across the room cried out. "Hallelujah!"

Keats was not one to be easily distracted. He replied, "Amen, Brother," then continued.

> Oh, Divine Master, grant that I may not so much seek
>
> To be consoled as to console,
>
> To be understood as to understand,
>
> To be loved as to love.
>
> For it is in giving that we receive
>
> It is in pardoning that we are pardoned,
>
> And it is in dying that we are born to eternal life.

I leaned toward Adrienne, but she put a finger over my lips. "Hush, Jack. You just hush."

Adrienne was correct. Discernment was a difficult proposition. Gray was now the color in fashion and only forgiveness was tolerated. I simply hoped Connor's jury would keep that in mind.

Sunday afternoons were quiet times for Adrienne and me. It was a time when I barbequed, and the two of us talked.

Adrienne seemed relaxed, somewhat pleased with herself as she sipped at her Dubonnet. I slit open a bag of Sparky charcoal, scooped the briquettes into a pyramid, and thought of ancient Egypt.

"I think Keats did rather well," she said.

"It wasn't what I'm used to. No fixed liturgy, no kneelers. Odd atmosphere. Catholic Masses don't have the same type of audience participation, or at least they didn't use to." Instantly I was sorry. It was wrong to say "audience"; "congregation" would've been better.

"The Amazing Grace is going to succeed, I'm sure of it. It's inclusive. People want that."

I began playing with the briquettes, flattening them on the bottom of the grill. "Let's hope so."

"I've invited Thomas Piggott for lunch. I didn't think you'd mind."

"When'd you do that?"

"You were bringing the car round after church. He was standing on the steps all alone." She popped up from her chair. "He should be here any minute." She reached for my glass, and her hand lingered against mine. "I'll make you another one."

She started toward the house then suddenly stopped. "Oh, Jack, look who's here."

I looked and saw Piggott on the steps. He waved. "Sorry if I'm a bit tardy. I stopped and bought beer."

"I'll be right back," Adrienne said. "Meanwhile you two can get to know one another."

She disappeared, and Thomas, bottle of beer in hand, made his way towards me. "Adrienne tells me you were in the Air Force."

"True."

"She mentioned you were in Japan."

"For twelve months."

"The architecture there is very important."

Japan was to me a country I had once been to and come back from and could never quite leave behind. What Piggott knew of Japan I didn't know and was not interested in listening to him relate. I could recall as if it were yesterday a group of women on a hillside kneeling in a stream washing clothes among the rocks. I could recall watching an old man, back bent low, pulling a wooden cart of firewood up a mountain road with no house in sight. Piggott would see Japan in his own way. Being the host, I answered as best I could. "I'm sorry. I know very little about architecture."

"Of course," he said ever so politely.

I turned the chicken and ribs. Piggott was a confident man with a good reputation. I didn't doubt he was good at his profession.

"No offense, Jack..." He stopped mid-sentence as if waiting for my okay to continue. "It's no secret you're representing Connor. What puzzles people is why. By now everyone in town has seen the tape of the shooting. How can you win such a case?"

"Perhaps he was justified in killing the man."

"What a strange attitude for an attorney."

I checked my temper. Piggott had but an architect's understanding of attorneys, and I should expect no more. And yet I intended to set him straight.

"Connor believes he was protecting his family. That's worth doing, don't you agree?"

He shifted his feet. "Is that what he was doing?

Adrienne popped between us. "Don't overcook the meat, Jack." She was right, the ribs were done and the chicken blackened. It was time we had lunch.

***

By ten fifteen I was lying in bed watching Adrienne undress. Overall the day had gone well. I had been successful in keeping in the good graces of my wife, and Piggott was finally gone. Taking the broader view, I was willing to admit there was little wrong with Piggott. He and I would never fly in the same flock, but he had been agreeable in his own way. He had eaten my barbecue and I had drunk his Dos Equis. It was a fair exchange. Something for something.

He was of the opinion that Connor should be convicted and that loyalty, in some matters, is a waste of time. What profit would there have been in arguing? He was an educated man who built expensive homes for well-thought-of people, and besides, my wife liked him. Had I chosen a different tack, would I be here watching my wife in a negligee turning her shoulders as she sat before a mirror? Why she moved about in such a fashion I never asked, for when she was done, she would allow her nightgown to slip from her shoulders, then step out, leaving herself covered only by two small pieces of silk.

Tonight was different. The nightgown slipped from her shoulders, but she remained seated, eyeing me in the mirror. "Mr. Fuller would like to see you tomorrow."

This was not good news. I had no wish to see Fuller, but neither did I intend to upset Adrienne. "Tomorrow is a busy day for me."

She reached behind her for the clasp on her bra and found it. "Margaret Fuller called."

I pushed my face into the pillow to hide but left a line of sight for one eye to watch her.

"Go see the man, Jack. It can't do any harm. Margaret thinks the two of you should have a talk."

I refused to answer, simply waited, taking my chances.

"Jack, I know you're not asleep."

She had me cold. I thought it best to answer. "When did Margaret call?"

"When I was inside making your drink. I worried about leaving you and Thomas alone for as long as I did."

I didn't like being worried over. "Maybe Thomas and I got along better than you imagine. I found him quite likable."

She gave me a half smile as though she knew I was exaggerating. "There was one other call. Some girl named Kathy who claimed to be a reporter for *The Advocate*. She was calling from Biloxi."

Why had Adrienne mentioned that Kathy had called from Biloxi? Was it possible one of our friends had seen us poolside at the Edgewater? It was something worth worrying about, but for now I was in business. Adrienne walked toward me, bare-breasted and willing.

Without warning she stopped. "Why was she calling?"

"Kathy keeps watch over the Connor Fund. She also arranges the talk shows."

"I hardly think she was calling from Biloxi about bookkeeping. Do you?"

"I won't know until I call her."

Without a moment's hesitation Adrienne turned off the light. "She doesn't have what I have. Does she?"

16

Satisfied with my Waffle House breakfast of bacon and eggs, I was choosing a chocolate mint, adding it to my tab, when Kathy called.

"Need to talk. Where are you?"

"At the Waffle House. You?"

"French railroad car."

"Finishing up now. Glad you called. Be right there."

After World War II, the French had shipped the car to Baton Rouge to honor the boys and men from Louisiana who had died on French soil fighting the Germans. It stood on the grounds of the Old State Capitol, surrounded by a handsome fence topped with fleurs de lis, and was fifteen minutes away.

I reached the traffic circle, held to the outside lane, and spun off towards the river and Kathy. She was sitting on a bench, phone to her ear. I gave her a happy honk of the horn. She rose with one quick motion, waved, and soon was seated beside me.

"Did Adrienne tell you I called?"

"She did. What's up?"

There was a spark in her eyes. "Do you know who Rebecca Wylie is?"

"She once covered the State Department for *The New York Times*...?"

"Right. *The Times* began downsizing and she took early retirement. That's how she ended up at *The Constitution*."

"I didn't know."

"The South is lucky to have her," Kathy said. "Last year she won the Goldsmith Prize for investigative journalism."

"Oh."

"Remember the corrupt U.S. Senator from Alabama who was forced to resign?"

"Okay."

Kathy smiled, poked me in the arm. "Rebecca wants an interview with both you and Connor."

I pulled in and parked at my favorite place to look at the river and the bridge. Kathy was someone I didn't want to disappoint. And yet... "I'm not letting Connor do any interviews. Sorry."

"Is it because of who she is? Be honest."

I thought it best to speak frankly. "She took down a U.S. Senator. What chance would Connor have?"

She fumbled with her phone. "What about you?"

I watched the river, wondering what my chances would be with Rebecca Wylie. No doubt she was skilled at questioning, probing here and there until she found a weakness, but what of it? I was good at this questioning business myself and might very well hold my own. I would admit to nothing, parrying her questions with questions of my own. The best I could hope for was a draw, but if it would help Kathy, it was a risk worth taking. First, I needed to make sure. "Would it help your career?"

"Doing favors for people like Ms. Wylie can't hurt."

"Okay."

Kathy was delighted, even seeing a way to benefit Connor. "I'll see to it she asks about the Connor Fund."

"Fine. When is she coming to town?"

She answered with a lilt in her voice, "She's already here. She was in New Orleans doing background work on police corruption in the Big Easy."

It mattered not, but I was curious. "Why is she interested in someone like Connor?"

She smiled. "She can explain that when we meet. Lunch is at Spagnola's at three thirty. They're keeping the restaurant open after hours. We'll be the only ones there."

"I'll be on time." I started the engine.

"It's only a block to *The Advocate*. I'll walk." She left the car with a bounce. It was clear she didn't wish to live out her life at *The Advocate*. If Kathy could walk, so would I. The parish jail was but a short distance from the river. I needed to check in on Connor.

***

I took the special elevator as usual. Lieutenant Trahan was on duty again. He waved me on as he punched open the lock. It clicked as I approached. The room always seemed to have a slight lingering of stale odors. Before long I heard the solid clanging of steel. Connor seemed tired, but he looked pleased to see me. "Any news? I'm hoping you have some."

"I'm afraid not. I just wanted to visit."

"Do you know when the trial will begin?"

"The District Attorney is anxious to have it over with, so it won't be long."

"That's good." His shoulders were slightly hunched. "I'm worried about Scot. Have you seen him?"

"No, I haven't." Trying to be optimistic, I said, "I'm sure he's fine."

"I want to see for myself."

"I don't know if Mary Beth would permit him to visit you in jail. Do you?"

"Can't you force her to?"

"It's got procedural problems. If I filed a motion in court seeking the judge's okay, her lawyer would file a motion to delay. Your trial would be over before the matter was resolved. I'm sorry. I always seem to be telling you no."

Suddenly his eyes brightened. "I know what. You could go by Scot's school. Bring him here. Mary Beth wouldn't know until it was too late."

Attorneys didn't do such things. We plied our trade in comfortable mahogany offices and wood-paneled courtrooms. We didn't scurry about the streets subverting judicial decrees. There was but one problem. I knew I could pull it off. Scot would be delighted to see his father. Then afterwards when I brought him home, Mary Beth would say nothing. No mother worth her salt would turn her son's happiness sour. And yet I had serious misgivings. Was I to become some go-between? Was this a prelude to what Connor would expect of me when he was in prison?

Connor pointed a finger at me. "If you're my friend, you'll go. He stays after school every day for basketball practice."

"What school?"

"Saint Agnes."

Was it a coincidence? I'd made my first communion at Saint Agnes. "On one condition."

"Sure, whatever you want." His eyes drifted downward. "I'm in no position to bargain with you."

"I want you to let me try the case my way."

His voice was flat. "You're the lawyer."

"No, listen to me. I don't want the jury to see you as an avenging angel. As the matter stands now, Pohl is the only victim. We need a victim on our side of the fence."

"I'm no victim."

"No, but Scot is."

His head jerked, his eyes turning hard. "Scot is not going to testify. I won't have that."

I'd expected this. "As an attorney, I have to put before the jury any evidence that might help you. Scot is the only person who can do that. He'll have to testify."

He rose halfway from his chair, looking down at me. "Don't make me angry with you, Jack."

"Sorry if I upset you, but you have to trust me. I want the jury to see you as they might see someone going off to war to defend their country. We have to get the jury to believe there was something honorable in what you did. Pohl has to be seen as an enemy who was a danger to society. I don't want the jury to see you as a person acting out of vengeance. Scot is the key to that. This is a matter of your life, Conner. You're a good man. You're no criminal, and you don't deserve to spend your life in a penitentiary. Don't forget that. There's still a chance I can get you off. Let me do what I think best."

"I don't like it, Jack. Yes, I want to protect Scot. That's true. That was the reason I shot Pohl. And that's why I won't allow you to put Scot on the stand. He's been through enough."

It was time to retreat. I had broached the subject, given him fair warning of what was to come. It was my duty as a lawyer to see that Scot testified. The judicial process demanded that I do so, but the most I could do for him now was to bring Scot to visit with him. I stood. "What you're asking is not particularly ethical but what the hell. Scot needs to see his father as much as you need to see him. I'll try to pull it off, but no promises."

17

Spagnola's was a cozy place with an L-shaped dining room, cane back chairs, and tables draped in oilcloth. Except for two waiters in bowties standing at a small bar, no one was about.

They knew me and I knew them, but none of us spoke. It was a game of sorts, perhaps their way of giving an air of dignity to their restaurant. The two of them eyed me for a time before the taller one addressed me. "You lookin' for someone?" He was the more dour of the two, a person who remained aloof no matter how generous the tip.

"Just waiting." Had Mr. Spagnola failed to mention us?

"We're closed. Don't open again until six."

"I know."

Satisfied he had dealt with me properly, he turned away, went back to drinking his beer.

Time passed, the kitchen door opened, and out came Mr. Spagnola in a long white apron. He gave no notice he had seen me, though I was positive he had, and went straight to a small wooden table beneath a poster of Venice. When he had paid the two of them their wages he spoke to me, his voice heavy with accent.

"You come here with *The Advocate*?"

"I'm a bit early."

He shook his head. "My mistake. I assume lunch for three ladies." He gestured toward a table. "You sit here. I bring you a cold beer."

It was clear why Mr. Spagnola had made a success. He was a generous host, a man happy to provide. He disappeared and then was back quickly with a bottle of San Miguel and a frosted glass.

"Waiters are gone now. The door is locked. If you will open the door for Ms. Postlewait, I go back to my kitchen."

The afternoon was not without its rewards. Like a celebrity who reserved a restaurant to enjoy his Sam Miguel in solitude, I studied the frost on my glass, admired the amber color of my beer. When the knock on the door came, I kept my end of the bargain with Mr. Spagnola and was soon peering into a bright afternoon sun, squinting with one eye at Kathy and Rebecca Wylie. She was dressed in beige, her dark hair covered with an emerald scarf.

How would this lady, come down from the eastern establishment, and I get along? She seemed detached yet friendly.

She looked me over while removing her sunglasses. "I'm pleased to meet you, Jack. It was good of you to come." She had a look around. "Lovely place...just darling."

Standing close beside me, Kathy gave me a playful poke in the ribs and whispered, "Isn't she nice?" I expected no less. After all, Ms. Wylie was a lady groomed and polished by years at *The New York Times*. Kathy headed for the kitchen. "I'll let Mr. Spagnola know we're here."

Ms. Wylie gestured toward a table. "You're involved in a compelling trial, Jack."

"If you're going to write about Connor, I'd like to know what viewpoint you'll be taking."

She took her time, folding her glasses neatly away into a soft leather case before responding. "There's always the sexist angle when a husband kills his wife's lover." She slipped the scarf from her hair, folded it neatly and placed it in her handbag. I wanted to interrupt, ask her what proof she had that an affair had taken place. But I didn't. No doubt she'd already spoken to the district attorney.

"We feminists loathe being seen as chattel," she said, "so we strongly resist the notion that a husband has a right to kill if his wife is having an affair. It's medieval. We've reached a measure of equality these days in that women have taken to killing their husbands when they transgress. Perhaps that's one reason I've chosen to move on from the subject."

Kathy returned with a happy glint in her eye. "Mr. Spagnola will be serving in a few minutes. The food looks wonderful." She took a seat beside Ms. Wylie. "So what are we talking about?"

Ever the gracious lady, Ms. Wylie turned her attention to Kathy allowing her eyes to linger a moment. "I was about to explain my interest in Connor's trial. It fits nicely with my plan to write a series of articles on the destruction of children in today's society."

Kathy shook her head. "It's terrible, isn't it?"

Ms. Wylie acknowledged the approval and continued with a cadence that prominent journalists perhaps take if expecting to be quoted or recorded. "This killing of children while they are at school is becoming a pattern. I don't believe it can be stopped completely. I believe the result will be a desensitization. An acceptance, if you will, as though such tragedies are inevitable. Then there's the killing of one's own children by the spouse who has been denied custody. Collectively I see this as a red martyrdom. But what of our children who're being destroyed by a white martyrdom? I believe they go unnoticed. Physical violence is awful, but emotional violence is too. Perhaps I can use Connor's story to alter that. This trial can be sensationalized because of the killing, but the real story is Scot and what becomes of him… what does that do to his life if he loses a father?"

I didn't like it. I would do my best to prevent the boy from becoming entangled in some consciousness-raising undertaking. "I don't wish to sound rude, but it appears I've come here under a pretense. Kathy said you wished to interview me. She didn't mention Scot."

Ms. Wylie remained cool as a cucumber. "I am interviewing you, Jack, but in my own way. In fact, I just learned a great deal about you."

She glanced at Kathy, then back at me. "Kathy can appreciate what I've done. And yes, I do need your help."

"What do you want from me?"

The kitchen door opened, and Mr. Spagnola came toward us, carrying a tray with glasses and a bottle of wine. Laying each glass before us with a practiced motion, he opened the bottle and poured a taste of it into Kathy's glass. "Verrocchio is very nice."

She sipped it. "It's perfect."

Mr. Spagnola smiled, poured wine into our glasses, said "Enjoy," and disappeared.

"You asked what I want of you, Jack," Rebecca said. "That's a fair question." She sipped her Chardonnay. "Tell me why you're defending Connor. You're not a criminal lawyer."

How was I to answer? Rebecca was looking for a story to tell, and I would help if I could. "We ran a paper route together for two years when we were in high school…delivered *The Advocate* in the morning before school on a motorbike. One morning he would drive and I would throw, then we would switch. Then there was the fishing. We fished on Saturdays."

She seemed pleased by my reminiscing, "And what of Mary Beth?"

"I like her. She liked me. We were good friends."

"And what of Scot?"

I shook my head, "I haven't seen much of the boy."

Before she could ask another question, Mr. Spagnola arrived. Balancing three small skillets on his forearm, he served stuffed pork chops, small potatoes, and slightly burnt green beans onto our plates. "Now you enjoy," he said and disappeared.

Kathy spoke first. "Isn't this delightful?"

Rebecca smiled. "Everything has been done quite handsomely."

I wondered what might have become of Mr. Spagnola had he remained in Italy. Surely the odds were against his owning an Italian restaurant. He had the arms of a farmer, thick and heavy, and I could picture him working the fields, stopping for his noontime lunch, enjoying a bottle of red wine and a roll of hard salami beneath a shade tree. Now that hardly mattered, for he had come to America for a new beginning and succeeded.

Ms. Wylie gave a tap of her fork and returned to her purposes. "In fairness to you, Jack, you should know I've spoken to the district attorney. He believes Connor's motive had to do with Mary Beth having an affair." She paused to look at Kathy. "She tells me you disagree."

I too looked at Kathy. "She's right. Connor had reconciled himself to the affair. It was the kidnapping."

"I see." She eyed me closely. "Wealthy children are kidnapped for ransom. Children like Scot are kidnapped for only two reasons. They're either used for sex or sold for snuff films."

"Connor is convinced his son was molested," I said. "He seems quite certain of it."

"Has Scot told him that's what occurred?"

"Connor can't be certain. He was arrested before there was any opportunity to speak to Scot. He'd only been home for a day before the shooting. Neither Connor nor Mary Beth wanted to make Scot talk about what had happened so soon."

I liked Ms. Wylie. She was a lady with credentials and knew her business. I thought it all to the good to speak of Connor, Mary Beth, and Scot. But what of Alfred Pohl? What sort of man had he been when he was alive? Pohl didn't strike me as a man who had suddenly gone sour. He'd come here out of nowhere, had an affair with a married woman, then kidnapped her son. The odds were he was a man with a past. I had requested information from the FBI and the Freedom of Information Act but so far had gotten no answer. This was typical, and I knew I had no way to force them to reply. He'd used aliases, which made it impossible for me to track him, as I needed locations to even begin trying to look over courthouse records or arrests. A fulltime detective and money would help, but I had no access to those, which is exactly why criminals such as Pohl get away with their acts. The police department wasn't interested because he was already dead.

"What of Mary Beth? Have you spoken with her?"

"Under the circumstances, no, I haven't."

Ms. Wylie seemed to sparkle. She turned to Kathy. "My plane to Atlanta doesn't leave until early evening. We should have time to drop in on Mary Beth. We can talk to Scot as well."

Kathy was happy to oblige. "I'll drive."

I didn't see things the way Kathy did. I wasn't going to let Ms. Wylie question the boy.

18

In spite of the chill, the young boys wore only white tee shirts and gray shorts as they ran their drill shooting layups. The red clay court was scuffed and pockmarked here and there from years of neglect. Standing near the iron-rimmed goal was a man dressed in a sweatshirt and the black gabardine pants of a Catholic priest.

I gave him a wave. "Hello, Father. May I speak to you?"

He gave three short bursts on his whistle, and the boys formed a circle around him. "Take a water break, form a line, and no shoving," he said sternly, then walked in my direction. "I'm Father Lieux. How can I help?"

"Jack Carney, Father. I'm representing Connor Padget in his trial and, with your permission, I'd like to speak to Scot."

"From what I've read in the newspaper, you're also a friend of Mr. Padget's."

"Yes, Father, that's correct."

He waved an arm. "Scot! Over here."

A boy, his blond hair matted down in sweat, came running. He was short for a fifth grader but had an athletic way of moving.

"This is Mr. Carney," the priest said. "He's come to speak to you about your father."

He waited to see Scot's reaction and then left us, going back to watch over the team break at the water fountain.

Standing before me the boy waited politely, his chest heaving in and out while he caught his breath. "Scot, I'm the lawyer who's helping your father." He didn't answer, simply stared up at me. "You know your father needs a lawyer, right?"

"I know what my father did. I don't know much about lawyers."

"I visited with Connor this morning at the jail. He wants to know how you're doing."

He shrugged. "I'm okay."

"Do you need anything?"

"I'm okay."

"Would you like to see him?"

His eyes filled with hope. "Can you do that?"

"Go change clothes while I ask Father Lieux."

Years ago, I'd been one of these boys. Brother Peter had spent his life as a Brother of the Sacred Heart and was our coach. I'd been lucky. Back then, I lived in a world that protected its children.

I thought back to my days at Sacred Heart. It was the winter of eighth grade and the first game of the season. I'd been dropped off early. The gymnasium was dark and empty, so I wandered between the gym and the red brick building where the Brothers lived. The principal's office was in the front, the first door on the left. I'd been there but once, a fact I was proud of, for those invited were there for a scolding. The rest of the building was given over to sleeping, eating, and relaxing for the Brothers.

A single exception was spoken of only by rumor. It was said that in the rear was a staircase that led to a private chapel.

Each morning a priest from St. Joseph's Cathedral would arrive at six o'clock and say Mass for the Brothers. I'd never seen such a thing as a private chapel and wondered what one would look like. I decided to check it out.

I studied the building carefully. There was but a single light burning in a top window, which likely meant no one was home. The thought gave me courage, and I tried the front door. It opened, and I went inside, walking quietly toward the rear of the short hallway in search of the chapel. The next door opened upon the sleeping quarters of the Brothers. Twelve single iron cots lay next to each other in two long rows. I had only seen such things in movies about the military. That was the moment I came to understand the Brothers lived like soldiers and had little thought for their own comfort. I went past the cots and tried the door in the back of the room. Finally, I had found the stairs. At the top was the chapel itself. An overwhelming peace settled over me. An immaculate white cloth covered the altar and, above it, hung a crucifix. To the left a sanctuary candle flickered softly, casting light over the room. I dropped to my knees, said a prayer to play well, and remembered to thank God ahead of time like the Brothers taught us. Then I went quietly back down the stairs. Outside, as I walked to the gymnasium, I pondered what had happened.

The sound of Father Lieux's whistle broke through the cold air and brought me back to reality. He walked over. "How was your visit? I saw Scot run toward the locker room, so I assume you came to take him home."

"Actually, I'm taking him to the jail to see his father. Connor asked that I bring him for a visit, and Scot was delighted. I assume it's fine with you."

"Of course. I'm pleased to see someone taking an interest in the boy's situation. Bless you, Jack, for helping the family. You can be assured I'll be at the trial each day and praying for you to do your best."

"Thank you, Father. It doesn't seem that long ago that Connor and I were playing basketball on this same court."

"Here comes Scot now." Father Lieux extended his hand toward me.

Scot came to a stop next to us with a twinkle in his eyes. "Thanks, Father. See ya tomorrow. I'm going to the jail to see my dad."

"Have a good visit."

I pointed to the Mustang parked at the curb "There's our ride. Should we put the top down?"

"Neat!"

We were nearing the jail without a word passing between us. It hardly mattered. Scot sat near the door and leaned out the car window, his face set against the wind.

"A very important lady is in town," I said. "I wouldn't be surprised if she isn't visiting your mother at this very moment."

"Who is she?"

"Her name is Rebecca Wylie. She works for a newspaper in Atlanta."

"Why is she talking to my mother?"

"She wants to write about your father."

"Is that good?"

"Hard to say. She may want to talk to you about what happened in Memphis."

"Mother told me not to talk about that."

"You should listen to your mother."

I disliked talking about private matters with strangers. These days, grief counselors were busy plying their trade among the sorrowful. Wasn't the love of a family member stronger than the wisdom of strangers? I turned left onto Park Boulevard. "Have you seen your father since you came back?"

"Just the day I got home. The next day he shot Mr. Pohl."

"You've never been in a jail. Do you think it'll upset you?"

"No, sir."

"Connor is anxious to see you." I slowed and turned into Couvillion's Easy Park. "The building on the corner, that's the courthouse. The jail is on the top floor. We'll take an elevator, go through a door, then we'll be in the jail. Okay?"

"Don't worry, I'll be okay. I'm getting to see my dad."

Lieutenant Trahan was at the duty desk reading, paying no heed to the sounds of the elevator opening.

"Afternoon, Lieutenant," I called out. "This is Connor's boy."

"No reason a son can't see his dad." He shut the book and waited a moment to put the boy at ease. "Son, you just follow Jack. I'll go find your dad."

In the attorney-client room, Scot and I sat quietly, waiting. Finally, Connor entered, and he didn't hesitate. He scooped up Scot in his arms. "Well, look what I have here." He held the boy for a time, then put him down. "You look fine. Just fine."

There was a shine in Scot's eye and a tear as well. When he spoke, I could barely make out the words, they were so softly spoken. "Are they going to let you come home?"

"When the trial is over." Connor ran his hands through the boy's hair. "Did you thank Mr. Carney for bringing you?"

I stood. "I'll be in the hall talking to the lieutenant. You two take your time."

* * *

When Scot and I reached the sidewalk outside the courthouse, the gray winter sky had not yet turned black.

"You live in Woodland Ridge, don't you, Scot?"

"On Horseshoe Bend Road."

The district attorney lived not ten miles from there on Harrell's Ferry Road. More than once I had gone to Benton's house after an LSU game. Sour mash bourbon in hand, I had walked his yard watching the shadows of smoke cast out from the flames of Hawaiian tiki torches. If LSU won, we felt good about ourselves, for the university was in a way home to us. There we had earned our bachelor's degrees, from there we went off to war, suffered the deaths of friends, and returned to study law.

Was it providence that I was within an easy drive to Benton's when Scot and I were already together? I couldn't be sure, but neither could I deny it might well be an omen.

"Scot, what time does your mother expect you?"

"It's dark when Father Lieux drops me off."

"Good. We have some time. I believe you could do with a present. Do you have a bicycle?"

"A three-speed. One Saturday I rode it all the way to Amite River."

"Must be at least five miles from where you live."

"I got lost twice before I got home, but I did it."

"There's plenty of woods and swamplands as I remember it. I used to go there myself to shoot snakes. You have to be careful though. Sometimes water moccasins will drop from a willow tree right on you when you're near the water."

"I'm careful." He shifted in his seat, began playing with the strap of his seat belt. "You don't need to buy me a present, Mr. Carney, you already took me to jail."

I glanced at him, studied his face. "No, I don't. But I don't want you to worry about your father. He's in trouble, and it's a lawyer's job is to see to it that a person's troubles are not as bad as they seem, okay?"

He turned his head and looked out the side window.

"That's why I'm going to make sure you're safe next time you go to the Amite.

An Easy-Buy electronics store was nearby, just two blocks off the Interstate, and in less than twenty minutes we were walking out the door with a set of yellow faced Motorola walkie-talkies with a range of thirty-five miles. "If you run into trouble," I said, "you can call home."

"That's neat. I haven't seen one before. Nobody I know has one."

Benton would enjoy this too. I was pleased with myself. Things were going better than expected. The kid was easy to be around.

Scot held the walkie-talkie set in his lap, running his fingers along the edges of the sealed plastic, pausing now and then to give the plastic a whump. The whumping noise was the only sound between us until I pulled into the Dixie Inn Chevron station.

"I don't know how to work a walkie-talkie," Scot said. "I've heard about 'em, but I've never seen anybody do it. Is it hard?"

"They're not just for trouble. They're fun too. Do you have a friend in your neighborhood?"

"Tommy. He's my best friend."

"I'll teach you some military language, that's the main thing about using 'em, and you can teach Tommy."

"My father said you were in the Air Force."

"That's true."

The Dixie Inn was awash in lights, a clean, bright place with computer-operated pumps. I gave the pump handle a squeeze, felt the hose jerk at the sudden surge of gasoline, and began to consider what I was doing. I needed to call Mary Beth to tell her I had Scot. Outside the service station, I pulled over to dial her number.

Her voice was as I remembered, friendly and appealing. "Mary Beth, this is Jack. I've been intending to call. How are you?" I was not surprised when she remained silent. "I apologize if I'm interrupting anything."

She answered, her voice flat, uninterested. "Why are you being so polite, Jack?"

"I have Scot with me. I hope you don't mind."

Her voice was no longer flat. "Of course I mind." She paused, then her tone changed. "And may I ask just why you have my son with you?"

"Connor asked for a visit. I drove by St. Agnes and basketball practice and picked him up."

"Did you take him to the jail? He's only eleven, for God's sake."

"He was thrilled with the idea. He had fun. He misses his father. It did him good."

"And how is his father?" She spoke in a voice that was without any hint of kindness.

"About what you'd expect. I'm at the district attorney's house now. We won't be long."

"Oh." She paused. "Do me a favor, will you? Tell the district attorney I'll leave the country before I testify. I'll go to Mexico if I have to."

"Has he subpoenaed you?"

"He has."

"I'll speak to him."

"When you're done, you bring Scot straight home."

"We won't be long."

"Wait, don't hang up." For a moment there was silence. I heard her breathe deeply. "If you're going to talk to the district attorney, there's something you should know."

"I'm listening."

"After the shooting an investigator from his office came to see me. He wanted a statement. He was certain Connor's motive for shooting Pohl was because of an affair. I told him that wasn't true, but he badgered me, and finally I just wanted him to go away. So, I signed a statement saying I did."

"The DA can force you to testify. You have no choice if he insists."

"I'll deny it. I'll say his people put pressure on me when I was upset. You tell him that."

"I'll do what I can. But you don't have to testify to anything except what you saw Connor do. You have a privilege as his wife that what he may've said to you before the shooting is private…between the two of you. You only have to answer to what you saw him do. If he showed you his gun and said, 'I'm leaving to shoot the man,' you don't have to tell the court what he said. But if he loaded a gun and left the house and you saw that, you're responsible to state it. I doubt you really have a problem with what you saw and what you have to say. I'll try to see what I can do to keep you away from testifying. It's not yet time to really deal with that."

"You get Scot back home soon and tell the DA I mean what I say."

I said goodnight and dialed Benton's number. After a single ring he answered. "Hello."

"This is Jack. I'm next door at the Dixie Inn."

"Come on by."

19

Upon arriving at Benton's I pried open the Motorola set. Learning how to properly use the walkie-talkie would help Scot pass the time while Benton and I visited. Scot was all ears. "In the Air Force when we flew, we used call signs. That's how we knew who we were talking to, so having a call sign is very important. Okay?"

"Yessir."

"Why don't you choose a call sign that has something to do with basketball."

"Okay, what?"

"What part of the game do you like best?"

He didn't hesitate. "When we run a fast break. That's fun."

"Okay. You can be Fastbreak One. How about that?"

"Okay. What are you going to be?"

"How about Outbreak Seven?"

"That sounds okay."

I held the walkie-talkie to my ear. "When you want to call me, the first thing you do is identify yourself. Start by giving your call sign. Next, you'll want to know if I heard you, so you use my call sign, which is what?"

"Outbreak Seven."

"Right. It's not hard is it? Next you need to know how well I can hear you. That's important, isn't it? You do that by asking, 'Do you read me?' If I hear you loud and clear like we're talking right now, I answer by saying either five by five or five square. Want to give it a try?"

He was smiling, enjoying the game we were playing. He held the walkie-talkie to his ear. "This is Fastbreak One calling Outbreak Seven. Do you read?"

"Fastbreak One, this is Outbreak Seven. I read you five by five. You've got it down, Scot. Now let's go see Mr. Jones. He's a nice man and a friend of mine. He has a big yard for you to play in. There are even some woods for you to explore. Just keep the walkie-talkie with you and I won't worry. Understand?"

"Yessir."

Seated on the patio, Benton and I sipped bourbon in the evening air. "I wasn't surprised you called, Jack. I'll be glad when all this is over. I do admire your fortitude."

"Now that you've met Scot, what do you think of him?"

"He seems like most boys his age."

"We've just come from visiting Connor."

Benton reached into his shirt pocket for a cigar, offered one to me.

"No thanks."

He took his time lighting his cigar, admiring the burning red coal he had created before answering. "That explains the walkie-talkies. They looked to be brand new, just out of the box."

"He rides his bike to the Amite. He'll have one now to leave at home with Mary Beth if he has trouble."

"You should be careful, Jack, not to get involved. Now what did you want to see me about?"

"I'm not quite sure. I was in the neighborhood."

Benton twirled the drink in his hand, ice cubes clinking against the glass. "You wanted me to see Connor's son."

What was clear to Benton was not clear to me. Scrutinizing one's own motives could be a perilous proposition. I had thought my presence had more to do with visiting Benton as a friend before we met as adversaries in the courtroom. But I said nothing of the sort.

"You've subpoenaed Mary Beth. She wants you to know that if you put her on the stand, she's going to deny any affair with Pohl."

His eyes flared a bit. "She's in the middle of a murder trial. She admitted the affair to one of my investigators. She even admitted Connor accused her of such, which gives him knowledge, which gives him motive." He flicked the ashes of his cigar. "Tell her for me it's damn stupid to threaten a district attorney. Damn stupid, don't you agree?"

"Motive's not an element of the crime, Benton. You don't need to prove motive for a conviction. You don't have to drag her through a scandal.

He nodded. "Legally, you're of course correct, but the jury's going to want to know what's so important to Connor that he decided to kill. My job is to make them as comfortable as possible voting to convict."

"The jury will see the television tape, Benton. That's all you need for a conviction. A victory for Connor would be for the jury to find him guilty of manslaughter instead of murder."

Benton shrugged. "The lady is going to testify. This entire conversation we're having can be introduced into evidence.

There's no attorney-client privilege here because you're not her attorney. You're just a friend. How will she look to a jury when it comes out she's threatened the district attorney with perjury?"

I smiled, took my time sipping Benton's bourbon. "You have a clear-cut case, Benton. The last thing you want is a distraction. If you put Mary Beth on the stand, she'll say your investigator bullied her. The jury won't like the idea that the DA's office goes around intimidating women in Mary Beth's situation."

He didn't choose to respond and a quiet developed. It lingered until finally broken by a fuzzy, squeaking sound coming from the walkie-talkie beside me.

"Outbreak Seven, this is Fastbreak One. Do you read?"

I had seen Scot disappear past the lights of the tiki torches and head for Benton's woods and was happy to hear his voice. "This is Outbreak Seven. Fastbreak One, I read you five square. Over."

"Hi, Mr. Carney, this is Scot. What do I say now?"

"Fastbreak One, do you wish to declare an emergency?"

"No sir, I'm fine. I found a creek. Mr. Jones's woods are nice. Over."

"Don't go too far, Fastbreak One. We'll be leaving soon."

"Roger that."

I held the walkie-talkie in my lap, watching Benton reach for the bourbon bottle and pour another glass. His eyes twinkled. "Reminds me of my army days. And yes, Jack, he's a cute kid. I can see why you like him."

Benton and I were temporarily at cross-purposes, and yet we shared an experience that was difficult to speak of. We were well versed in the coexistence of the fear of dying mixed with a sense of indestructibility. It was a common emotion in our squadron to fly our missions knowing we would surely return and yet wondering if this was the time our luck would run out.

I said nothing, intent on keeping my memories to myself.

"Somehow, Jack, I never quite got used to coming back. We were young men who saw people die for their country. Now we see people die over nothing more important than sex or money." One of Benton's shoulders drooped as he spoke. He had been district attorney for twenty years, and it was telling on him.

"Honestly, Benton, you're wrong about Connor. He didn't shoot Pohl because of Mary Beth's infidelity. He was convinced Pohl had molested his son." I leaned forward. "Personally, I don't think he did. It doesn't quite make sense, does it? A man sleeps with the mother, then molests the son?" I sipped at my bourbon and wondered. Anything was possible these days and logic was no guide to human behavior. Ms. Wylie might have been onto something, and I decided to try it out on Benton. "Who knows? Maybe he was going to sell the boy for a snuff film."

Benton scoffed. "I don't care if Connor suspected the moon is made of cheese. None of these theories matter. Under Louisiana law Connor is guilty of murder."

I did not wish to quarrel and yet heard myself saying, "I wonder what I would have done if I were Connor. I wonder about that."

Benton shook his head. "Jack, I'm not going to follow you down some rabbit hole of moral relativism. It matters not a whit to me what either you or I would have done if we were Connor. It only matters what Connor did, and the matter ends there."

"You and I are friends, Benton, and yet we're going to court against each other."

"Brother against brother. It's happened before. Remember Antietam?"

"The South called it the battle of Sharpsburg."

Benton laughed. "Couldn't even agree on the name where all the killing took place."

"No, and yet the night after the first day of battle they sang to each other across the river."

"The Northerners had a band as I remember. Sounds odd maybe, but they did, and the band was playing Yankee songs, while on the other side of the river the Confederates were silent, just listening. Finally, when there was a lull, the Southerners yelled out for the band to play Dixie. And they did, and both armies sang the words together."

"Yeah, and when the sun came up, they went back to work killing each other for the second day."

"Strange story isn't it, but then we humans are an odd lot sometimes."

I turned to look at the sky. The air was getting cooler, and Scot would soon need a flashlight. I reached for the walkie-talkie on the table by my drink. "Mary Beth will be worrying if I don't get Scot back home on time."

"Yes, Mr. Carney, you have things to do."

I punched in to Scot. "Fastbreak One. Terminate mission and return to base. Over."

His reply was immediate. "This is Fastbreak One. I'm heading in."

***

Scot and I rode in silence. I was reluctant to bring up what had happened in Memphis, but this might be the only time we were alone. "Benton Jones is a nice man. Don't you think?"

He didn't respond. It was as if I hadn't spoken. I tried again. "You had a good time, didn't you?"

"Why did we go there?"

"Well—it's hard to say. Benton's an old friend. We're on the same team as lawyers, but we're against each other this time. That's how the legal system works."

"Weird. Think you can beat him?"

"I do. I think the law is on my side. That's what it's all about. And I'm younger than he is too. He's a bit worn down with age now. But he's still tough. I have to be prepared best I can."

"That's how you'll get my dad back home again?"

"That's how. Now come to think of it, I need to ask you some questions. You can help me."

"Okay." His mood had changed. Minutes ago, he'd been a boy with a sense of adventure. Now he was beginning to understand his father was in trouble. "Going home isn't the same anymore. It's just me and mother. I want my father back home. I miss him."

"That's something you have to understand. Connor may not be coming home again for a good while."

He made no reply, just gazed out the car window.

I pressed on. "Do you mind if we talk about Pohl? You might tell me something that'll help with the case."

"What do you want to know?"

"Why didn't Pohl bring you home when the tournament was over?"

"Mr. Pohl was doing business. He was on the phone a lot. He was waiting for some friends to come to Memphis."

"Did he ever say anything about you when he was on the phone?"

"He would go outside so I couldn't hear."

"You never heard anything?"

"One time I heard him say I was eleven."

"You eventually spoke to Mary Beth. How did you manage that?"

He began raising and lowering the window as he told his story. "I waited until Mr. Pohl went to town. Then I left. We were in a house out in the country, so I walked down the dirt road. Once I got on a bigger road, a man in a pickup truck stopped and gave me a ride. He dropped me off at the Quik Pak, and the lady there let me call Mom. She said for me to stay there and she'd have the police come bring me home."

A few blocks from Scot's house, I slowed the car. "What I'm going to ask you is very important, Scot. Did Pohl ever hit you, push you around, or do anything that you were afraid about?"

He stopped his playing with the car window and looked me straight in the eye. "No, sir."

I was relieved at his answer, but if Pohl didn't molest Scot, what Pohl had been up to was more sinister. A man like Pohl would seek to cover his footsteps. The police report only gave the facts about Scot's rescue. The police knew that Scot was expected home on Sunday. Pohl had claimed in the report that he'd misplaced his phone and was upset the boy was missing. None of this was proof of Pohl's past and didn't do more than set up a mystery.

"Did Mr. Pohl ever say why he wasn't coming back Sunday night like expected?"

"He said he was waiting for some friends who were bringing him some money. He talked to them on the phone. They were late."

Connor had shot the only man who knew the answer.

I pulled the car to the curb. "Tell Mary Beth we had fun together, and remember, carry the walkie-talkie with you when you go off on your bike. She won't have to worry about you that way."

"I promise." He held up the walkie-talkies and grinned. "I'm Fastbreak One now." He gave a quick salute with it. "And thanks, Mr. Carney, for taking me to see my dad."

"Good-night, son. I enjoyed it too. We've both had a nice day."

He disappeared through the front door, the walkie-talkies tucked under his arm.

Connor had been onto Pohl from the beginning. He'd taken Pohl for a wanderer, a stranger who appears suddenly among us, takes what he can, then disappears. It was an odd case: the father tries to save his son, and the son is the only one who now can save his father. I had new hope I could pull this off. Scot was an unusually bright kid.

20

Five years ago Adrienne and I had eaten our first meal at Robichaux's, a small place which at that time offered oysters and the coldest draft beer in the city. The restaurant had grown, and now the menu offered seafood of all types. While it still served cold beer, it also served the coldest martinis in the city.

Today we'd come for lunch, a time to be together. Adrienne sat across from me. Her cheeks had a soft glow, a sign she was happy.

"The martinis here are wonderful." She sipped from the wide stem glass.

"I'm glad you're happy, Adrienne. I know I've been something of a worry to you."

"It's been some time since we've been to lunch—and yes, I've missed that."

"It's the trial."

"Let's don't talk about that."

"You're right. Do you remember when you ate your first raw oyster?"

She smiled. "Raus's in New Orleans. I remember it clearly. We'd been to the races at the Fairgrounds. We were celebrating your having won the final three races."

"No one can do that, but that day I did."

She laughed. "We were young. You thought you could do anything. I would never have eaten those raw oysters if you hadn't been so lucky."

"You even ordered a second dozen."

"Now I love Rockefeller, but only when we eat at Antoine's. I order Bienville everywhere else." She reached for the salt shaker, turned it in her hand as though telling someone's fortune. "I think we were happier then. Do you?"

"We had our future in front of us in those days. Now we're in the middle of it and can't be sure how things will end."

"You're a success, Jack. That should count for something. Fuller, Bright, and Swayze is at least among the two best law firms in town. And you made partner quicker than most."

"What you say is true."

She reached for my hand. "Let's not be serious, Jack. I'm in the mood to enjoy life. And I've got a secret."

"I've got a secret too."

"You first, Jack."

"You're going to have two dozen yellow roses waiting for you when we arrive at our car."

Her eyes danced but then turned skeptical. "But how?"

"I made arrangements with Jimmy Clayton's florist shop. I'll call him when we order dessert, and he'll have a delivery man waiting for us at the car."

"Jack, you're such a character."

"Now your secret."

"Lately I've been doing a lot of reminiscing about my childhood." She spun the olive in her martini then lifted the glass. "You're right. These martinis are the best."

"Don't change the subject. Tell me your secret."

"I've been thinking about Blackie."

"The horse your father gave you for your twelfth birthday? The one that bucked you off?"

"You remember. I like that."

"You rode him in the mornings—before school."

"He didn't like it. That's why he'd buck me off. The odd thing was it didn't hurt."

"Where is all this leading?"

"I've been shopping for a horse. I want to learn dressage riding. It's a hobby lots of women enjoy. I've found a man who offers classes. His place is only a thirty-minute drive from our new house."

I hesitated. It would be poor form to take the edge off her mood, but I didn't intend to be dragged into a conversation about her West Indies house. This was a day for politeness. "Appaloosas are nice—gentle too. Have you decided on a breed?"

"I've been researching Andalusians. They're quite famous as you know, but it's hard to find a gelding, and I don't want a mare. There's a French breed that's popular now too. But they're all black and harder to ride."

The waiter appeared, set down a plate of Bienville before Adrienne and, before me, a plate of fried oysters. He was middle-aged and spoke in a pleasant voice. "I don't want to intrude, but are you the attorney, Jack Carney?"

"I am. Can I help you in some way?"

"No sir. It's me that wants to help you."

"In what way?"

"I saw you on TV. I have three boys and a girl. I worry over them. I worry something could happen to them. Like what happened to that Padget boy."

"I appreciate your concern. I'll need people like you on the jury."

He reached for his wallet. "Here's three tens. I want to give it to the Connor Fund—you can add to that whatever tip you were going to leave me."

"You're very generous."

"Cedric Blackwell. Wish I could do more."

"Thank you, Cedric."

Adrienne watched the waiter, waited until he was far away and not able to hear us. "I just learned two things, Jack. The first is that we have a very nice waiter who cares about what happens in our world, and secondly I have a somewhat famous husband."

I shrugged. "I guess more people than I thought watch *Midday in Louisiana*."

"I'm surprised at myself. I enjoy the idea of your becoming slightly famous."

"Fuller doesn't agree with you. He hates the publicity."

"Fuller is wrong. Still, I wish none of this had happened."

She reached for her fork and picked up one of her oysters. "These are perfect. I'm so glad we came."

We ordered desserts and coffee, and I dialed the florist. I was glad we had come, too. We'd had a good time together. "The roses will be waiting by the time I pay the bill and we walk to the car."

She smiled. "This has been lovely, Jack. I'm almost afraid to leave."

"Just remember one thing."

"What's that?"

"I love you. You know that."

"Does that mean you approve of my horse idea?"

"Of course, learning dressage fits you perfectly. I can't wait to see your horse when you buy it. But of course you'll have pictures before that."

21

I felt a wave of familiarity as I turned the Mustang into the driveway of Alvin's ranch-style house which also served as his law office. Alvin Dobbs was a criminal lawyer, and I knew him well. The land surrounding the house was large and well-kept with beautiful pecan trees. The two in the rear were near a swimming pool and offered welcome shade in the summer.

The solarium was my favorite room. It overlooked the swimming pool and was the place you could find Alvin when he wasn't in his office. I first visited there when I was about to graduate from law school. At the time, I was considering the possibility of establishing my own practice. Alvin rented three rooms to lawyers, and I'd heard there was a vacancy. I liked Alvin, the rent was reasonable, and I thought seriously of beginning my life as a lawyer there.

Then Fuller called with an offer. The salary was generous and came with the promise of a partnership within a year or so if things went well. I remembered my call to Alvin when I told him of my decision. His answer had been polite but came with a warning. He thought Fuller to be a harsh and structured man with no compassion.

Over the years, we'd kept in touch. He asked me to join his semi-annual poker game, which I happily did. What might have been had I begun my practice here? I made my way through the front door and to his secretary's desk. "Afternoon, Betty. I believe Alvin is expecting me."

She looked up from her work and smiled. "Go right in, Mr. Carney."

I headed through the double door to Alvin's office. He was neither on the telephone nor dictating but stood gazing onto the solarium. When he turned I could see he was dressed as always: a pinstriped wool suit and a dark charcoal vest. Strung across his vest was the gold Phi Beta Kappa key which he had earned at Tulane and always wore.

He appeared genuinely glad to see me. "It's been a while, Jack."

"I appreciate your allowing me to use your library. I've gotten myself into a hard case. I need to be more comfortable with the criminal side of the law, so I came to do research and get more familiar with how it works. Afterwards, I'd sure like to hear your advice. I'm up against Benton."

"No problem. On the phone you said you were defending a friend. Do you think that's advisable?"

"Can't be helped. He doesn't have the money to hire someone like you."

He shook my hand. "When you finish we'll talk and have a Ramos Gin Fizz in the solarium."

I was grateful to have Alvin as a friend. He was good at his trade, and I looked forward to what he might have to say.

He possessed one quality I thought necessary for anyone who chose to practice criminal law. He was an iconoclast. He started his practice in New Orleans with a prominent law firm, with branches in five major cities. Instead of thriving in the rarified air of the wealthy, he became bored. Against his family's wishes, he moved to Baton Rouge, set up a criminal practice, and became famous. Yet he didn't abandon civil work altogether. He liked to keep his hand in that side of things too, and when the chance came along to sue a big insurance company, Alvin could be who they were up against.

It was a disappointing search at first, but two hours later I came across The State of Louisiana v. Creswell. It was just what I needed. Doctor Creswell was a heart surgeon at the renowned Ochsner Clinic in New Orleans. Having drowned his wife in the bathtub of their upstairs bedroom, he was put on trial for murder in the first degree. What caught my eye was the jury found him guilty, but not of murder. Instead they had returned a verdict of manslaughter.

In his closing argument to the jury, Creswell's attorney had wasted no time in attacking the deceased wife.

> Doctor Creswell was a brilliant surgeon but was foolish when it came to women. It was she who had approached him in the bar in the Fairmount Hotel. He was relaxing with a scotch and soda after having addressed his peers at a medical convention in San Francisco. She lied to him from the beginning. She did not tell him she was a dancer at the Silver Slipper, a men's strip club. Instead she pretended to be the divorcee of

a Silicon Valley executive. She wrote to him some two months later saying how much that night had meant to her. She admitted she felt a strong sexual attraction toward him and wondered if they shouldn't meet in Barbados to see where things might lead.

The doctor was flattered and even kept the letter. Embarrassed as he was, he read the letter to you when he testified. You remember the difficulty he showed when he did so. He was a brilliant man publicly admitting he was also a fool.

But the letter worked, and after a week in Barbados the two were married, and the strip club dancer moved to New Orleans, the wife of a wealthy surgeon. She was a patient wife. She waited three years before she poisoned him.

She decided to kill him with arsenic, and if the doctor had not been born with a weak stomach, instead of testifying from the witness stand, he would be in a cemetery. Because of his stomach condition, he had bouts of diarrhea from time to time and so would have thought little of the attacks from the arsenic she was slowly feeding him. It was not until his urine became mixed with blood that he had tests run. That's when he knew the truth. He had arsenic in his system.

> He knew his wife was out to kill him. He had a moral decision to make. Doctor Creswell had taken an oath to save lives. In fact, he'd completed over fifteen hundred open heart operations without losing a patient. In the end, he decided he would prevent his wife from killing again after he divorced her, for surely she would search for another man of wealth and try again.
>
> So, right or wrong, Doctor Creswell decided to make sure that never happened. He took it upon himself to remove this woman who would kill for money.
>
> I ask you now to think carefully about what the good doctor did. Think very carefully. If he is set free to continue saving lives, how many lives will he save? At the same time weigh how many lives will be lost if he's imprisoned. Your responsibility is to balance the scales. That's all I ask. Consider carefully this man's life work. Perhaps he will be the recipient of compassion. I truly hope so.

My research ended. I could do no better. In criminal cases it was imperative for the lawyer to convince the jury the defendant had acted reasonably, that he was justified in his actions. Creswell's lawyer had done his job.

I made my way from the library, past the secretary's empty chair. It was just after five thirty. Was it an omen of sorts that this time of day and my life seemed to be crossing? An afternoon shade filled the solarium, and I spotted Alvin, his back turned, standing at the bar. A group of rattan chairs, placed in a semicircle around a glass coffee table, looked out on a small garden. It was an inviting setting. Alvin had taken no notice of my arrival. He remained busy preparing Ramos Gin Fizzes.

I spoke, but not so loud as to startle him. "I found a case I like."

"Good, we'll discuss what you've come across. Meanwhile take a seat." He finished with the gin fizzes and came to sit beside me, handing over my drink. "What I'd like to know first, Jack, is how you accomplished working with a man like Fuller all these years."

I laughed. "Fuller doesn't like you either. He still brings up that case he tried against you. The one where the two college boys from Tennessee were killed on their drive to New Orleans for Mardi Gras."

"Oh yes. They ran up the back of a semi truck in the fog."

"Fuller claims you're ill-tempered," I said.

"But of course he would. The man has no sense of drama." He stopped for a moment to sip his drink, then went on. "The jury awarded twenty thousand dollars, ten thousand for each boy, because they bought Fuller's argument that the accident had been mostly the boys' fault. When the verdict was read, I threw my glasses on the floor and yelled, 'I could get more for a dead pig!'" He laughed. "It did cause quite a stir."

"What about those glasses? I've never seen you wear them unless you're at trial."

"Glasses add a bit of sincerity. There's no prescription in the lens, and the people at Pearle Vision give me a discount."

I sipped my drink. "You have a point." It was as excellent as any drink I could remember. "And the gold Phi Beta Kappa key. What point are you making with that?"

"I'm quite proud of it, but that's not why I wear it." He seemed to think for a moment. "It brings a bit of class to my work. I like the notion of showing so-called elite attorneys I'm their intellectual equal." With a finger he traced the Phi Beta Kappa key and looked up at me. "You have a good reputation, Jack, but the word is out you're defending someone who shot a prisoner in handcuffs being returned to stand trial. As smart a trial lawyer as you may be, the criminal courtroom is no place for someone who makes his living defending insurance companies. Criminal courtrooms are dirty back alleys. Or at least they can feel that way to the uninitiated."

"Connor and I have been friends since high school."

He shifted his gaze. "You found a case that might be helpful?"

"The Creswell case. It originated in New Orleans."

"I know Doctor Creswell. He once saved a relative of mine. A second cousin but a relative nevertheless." He paused. "I believe he was defended by Bo Simoneaux. Got him off with manslaughter and, as I recall, the jury requested the judge show leniency in sentencing. Served something like five years. Now he's back practicing at Ochsner's." He held up his glass as if toasting. "I hope you'll be able to do the same for your client. Trials are tilted when the jury is selected. The facts of a case are important, but what is key is how a particular juror will see those facts. My name for that is politics. Connor used a gun for his killing, and gun ownership is highly political. In that regard you're in luck because you'll have a Southern jury. Don't let a Northerner on the jury."

THE TRIAL OF CONNOR PADGET

My thoughts went back to the interview with Ann Doherty. She'd asked me if I owned a gun. My instincts had kicked in and, while I hadn't lied, I avoided the truth. I didn't tell her there was a gun in the night table beside my bed and a Derringer in a shoebox in the downstairs coat closet. "Let's get back to the Creswell case. It gives me some hope."

Alvin leaned forward, placed his drink on the coffee table. "Indeed, I agree, but there are certain differences in Connor's case that you'll have to deal with."

"Connor's motives are confusing. That's going to be a problem for a jury. He's convinced this guy, Pohl, was sleeping with his wife. He even moved out and took an apartment. Then came the kidnapping, and Connor just lost it. He saw Pohl as an intruder who came into his life and wrecked his family."

"First his wife, then his child. That's a lot to endure... And you, Jack, you sound as if you aren't quite certain Pohl was having an affair with the wife. I notice these things. You said *Connor* was convinced. You didn't say Mary Beth *had* an affair."

"Very observant of you, Alvin. I'm not at all convinced, and I haven't quite figured out how to play it."

He shifted in his chair. "About justification. Be careful. Don't let it lead to Connor appearing arrogant or jealous. Avoid that. He should be seen as a man upon whom fate has thrust a burden too heavy to bear. A man ruined by events he had no control over."

"That's my big problem. I've seen little regret from him." An unexpected thought occurred. "There might be a way after all. If there is a way, it would be through his son. Connor has a soft side, and he loves Scot. If I were to keep Scot on the stand testifying, it would affect Connor. The jurors will see the strain it creates."

"That could build sympathy. Forget worrying about the affair. You stick to what you're able to prove, which is the kidnapping. Keep the jury's focus on Pohl." He stood and walked to the bar. "Let's have another, shall we?" He reached for the bottle of gin. "A proper Ramos Gin Fizz must be shaken and stirred for twelve minutes. It's worth remembering that tip. You never know when you might need one." He grinned and waved the shaker at me.

22

Midafternoon, and Adrienne was playing tennis. I was at my desk making a list of the questions Benton would probably ask Mary Beth. The phone rang. It was Mary Beth.

"Jack, I'm so glad you answered. If you hadn't, I was going to call the sheriff."

"What's happened?"

"It's Scot. He's hurt and needs help."

"Where is he?"

"In the woods along the Amite River that the boys go to. He called on the walkie-talkie."

"I know the place. Is he badly hurt?"

"He sprained his ankle chasing some boys who stole his bike."

"He just needs someone to bring him home. I can do that."

"Oh, thank you, Jack. I worry about him every time he goes off to those woods he loves so much."

"Did he tell you where on the river he was?"

"He's on the bank where the swimming hole is. The one with the swing rope hanging from a tree."

"Connor and I used to go swimming there. Call him and tell him to stay near the bank. I'll be coming from the river. No need for me to go through the woods."

"Thank goodness you were home."

The pirogue I used for duck hunting on Pecan Island was in the garage. It took only a minute to hook the boat trailer to the Mustang. Soon I was on I-10 headed for an abandoned church on Hobson's Road. The Church of Our Savior was a marker used to reach Hobson's Landing, and in less than thirty minutes I was there.

Using the boat ramp, I slid the pirogue into the water. Here and there the waters of the Amite ran shallow, but my flat-bottomed pirogue was built for such, and the paddling was easy. Almost immediately I felt at home. The trees were taller, and the switch cane growing in the water was thicker, but the feeling of being on the Amite was the same. As I reached the second bend in the river, the waters began to run shallow, and I steered more than paddled. Five minutes later I was back in safe water.

The Amite ran straight now, and I saw the rope hanging from the tree before I saw Scot. He was grinning and waving, but, as I drew closer, I could see he was standing with his weight on his right side. The bank was low, almost level with the river, and I guided the pirogue there. I reached for a bush and held the boat steady against the bank.

"You've had quite an adventure, haven't you?"

"Hi, Mr. Carney. I don't have a bike anymore."

"We'll talk about that later. For now, hop in while I hold the boat steady." After he eased himself in, I asked, "Let me have a look at that ankle." He propped it at an angle. "It's definitely swelling. We'll stop at a drugstore on the way home and get a support wrap and some ice."

"It hurts but not real bad."

I turned the pirogue toward Hobson's Landing and began to paddle. "Your dad and I used to come out here."

His eyes twinkled a bit. "My dad says you're good friends."

"We are. When we were younger, we came to this very swimming hole. A couple of times we came out here with your father's dog to hunt possum. We had some luck too."

"That sounds neat."

"We never came alone. You shouldn't either. You shouldn't come here unless you have a friend with you. Okay?"

"Tommy and I usually come together, but today he had to go somewhere with his parents."

"And look what happened."

"Yeah, I'll be more careful now. I'm lucky you could come get me."

We were approaching the shallows, and I dipped the paddle into the river sideways and began to steer.

"What else did you and dad do?"

"We sort of grew up together. We played sports on the same team. We went fishing together. We even went into business together with a paper route."

"Tommy and I are a lot like that. We do lots of things together."

"Would you like to paddle? I've got an extra one."

He beamed. "Sure. Looks fun."

I handed him the other paddle. "You do the left, and I'll do the right. We can stay straighter that way."

"Mr. Carney, can I ask you a question?"

"Go ahead."

"When are you going to bring my dad back home?"

"I don't really know, Scot. But I do know I'm going to need your help."

"What can I do? I'm only eleven."

"You can be a witness. You can tell the jury what happened in Memphis. They need to know, and you're the only one who can tell them. You're the only one who was there."

"You mean how Mr. Pohl wouldn't let me call home? How I had to run away?"

"Yes, all that. You can also tell them about how Pohl was waiting for some people to bring him money. They need to know all that."

"It all happened that way, okay. It's not hard to remember."

"Have you ever watched a trial on TV?"

"No."

"Well, you simply go to what we call a courtroom. There's a judge there and a jury. I'll be there too, of course. I'll ask you questions, and you just answer."

"What's a jury?"

"The people who decide if you're telling the truth or not. You can look at me the whole time you're telling your story. You don't have to look at them while you talk."

"When am I going?"

"I don't know yet. I'll tell your mother when it's time. There's something else you should know…I think you can get your bike back."

He stopped paddling and stared with amazement. "I never saw those boys before. And they're gone now."

"I'll bet the deputy sheriff knows just about everybody who goes in and out of these woods. I bet he's even seen you a time or two."

"Huh?" He squinted up at me, shading his eyes from the sun.

"It's their job to know what's going on out here. You give them a description of your bike, and I have a hunch they can get it back."

"Gosh, I sure hope so."

"Have your mom call the sheriff's office. She just has to tell them what your bike looks like and give a description of the boys. Things like—how many were there and how they were dressed. Within a couple of weeks, you'll have that bike back."

"Wow."

Hobson's Landing came into sight, and I stopped paddling to check my watch. It was two hours now since Mary Beth's phone call. Soon this afternoon would have run its course. It was an easy rescue of Scot this time.

"We need to call your mother. Do you still have the walkie-talkie?"

He reached inside his jacket. "Got it right here. I keep it on my belt with a clip." He flipped the switch, grinned at me, and said. "This is Scot, Mom. Do you read me?"

Mary Beth must've answered at once because, almost immediately, he said, "I'm with Mr. Carney. I'm okay. We're almost back at the landing now."

***

I placed two bottles of San Miguel beer on the patio table. Beside them I laid out Adrienne's favorite snack, a plate of cream cheese topped with Pickapeppa sauce. My timing was good, for minutes later I heard the noise of her car in the porte-cochere.

"I'm home!" She came smiling down the steps to the patio.

"I've fixed a surprise."

"How nice, my favorite."

"I even stopped by the liquor store for the San Miguel."

"That was sweet of you. Now ask me how I played." She seemed quite pleased with her day.

"How did you play?"

"I played Marcie three games. Won two and lost one."

"Was she upset?"

"No. Thank goodness, she's not like that. But she did accuse me of taking lessons."

"Did you have drinks afterwards?"

"With Tom Fenton and his wife. That's part of my news."

"Which is?"

"He wants you to become a member of the Louisiana Club." She nibbled a bit of cracker topped with cream cheese.

"Tom thinks the world of the Louisiana Club. I have my doubts."

"Oh, Jack, you should join. It's so much more acceptable than going to the Gunga Din."

"The Gunga Din's more convenient. It's only three blocks from the office."

"The right sort of people aren't at the Gunga Din. They go to the Louisiana Club."

The lights lining the flowerbeds turned themselves on as sundown settled in. "Those beds we planted look really pretty in the lights," I said. "Remember the weekend we spent doing all that work? It was worth it." I stood and walked over to the flowers for a closer look.

"Yes, they turned out great. It sets off the patio and the view from here is perfect. You should at least call Tom and thank him for the invitation."

"You're right, it would be rude not to. A person like Connor would never be invited to join. Is that the reason I should thank him?" I raised my beer in hand and, in my best voice, began to recite.

> The Northern lights have seen queer sights,
>
> But the queerest they ever did see
>
> Was that night on the marge of Lake Lebarge
>
> I cremated Sam McGee
>
> Now Sam McGee was from Tennessee,
>
> Where the cotton blooms and blows
>
> Why he left his home in the South to roam…

Adrienne clapped. "Our first date! We were driving by the university lakes. You recited the entire poem, and I was quite impressed."

"Well, that recitation of the Robert Service poem was brought to you by way of Connor Padget. He taught it to me."

She sipped at her beer. "It made you interesting. I'll admit I was quite taken. I always wondered what you might do next."

"Next, I introduced you to Rudyard Kipling, remember?"

She smiled. "So that's it. That's why you and Connor drink at the Gunga Din."

I sat down again in my chair. "If so, it's an unconscious thing. We never mentioned it."

"You're a better man than I, Gunga Din." She spread another cracker with cream cheese. "That's the line everyone remembers, isn't it?"

"Most people don't know Gunga Din was an Indian water boy hired by the British for the soldiers on the front lines. He was why they could keep fighting—Kipling wanted to honor that."

She put aside the cracker she hadn't eaten. "Aren't you doing the same thing, defending Connor? The boy sacrificed his life for the soldiers, and you're throwing away your career defending Connor. My God, I never realized any connection before."

"What I'm doing is not so great, Adrienne. I'm simply refusing to abandon a friend."

"Which brings me to my other news. Jeannette Fuller was at the club today." Adrienne reached into the pocket of her tennis jacket. "The firm sent you a check for $2,500 for the Conner Fund. It comes with a condition—you're not to cash it unless you'll rejoin the firm when this trial is over."

Adrienne held up the check, expecting me to take it, and I did. I looked for the signature and saw that Owen Swayze had signed it. Fuller could have put his name to the check, but he hadn't.

"Money buys things, Adrienne. That's mostly what money's good for. What's your opinion? Is this money meant to help Connor or buy me?"

A look of alarm arose in her eyes. "Oh, Jack, don't. This is not the time for you to be stubborn. You know exactly what this money represents. It's a peace offering. A gesture from a proud man. You have to take it."

I shook my head. "If I go back to the firm it won't be because they apologized with money."

"Oh, Jack. Just this one time. Please don't."

I opened her hand, laid the check in it. "It's their money, Adrienne. Give it back to them."

23

Adrienne was upstairs taking a bath and getting herself primed for her march on the Amazing Grace Chapel. When last I looked, she had lit two honeysuckle-scented candles near the vanity basin. I liked the smell of them myself, and she said it was a popular new idea everyone was doing.

I was downstairs, having escaped to my cubbyhole den, where I lay stretched out on the oak floor in front of my thirteen-inch Sony television. It was eleven o'clock, and I could catch the start of ABC's *This Week with George Stephanopoulos*. He was a favorite of mine, and today I had gotten double lucky. One of his guests was Donna Brazile who was raised right down the road in New Orleans. She was solid and dependable and could compete against Ann Coulter, another good choice for today. Ann, with her long hair, was an attention getter, and Donna would have to be on her game.

It would be a show worth the watching and would fill the time nicely until Adrienne and I set off for the Amazing Grace Chapel. Stephanopoulos began earnestly enough. He acknowledged his guests in his cocky yet friendly way, then got down to business.

He stared directly into Donna's eyes and began. "This morning we will be raising awareness of the plight of our nation's children. Sixty-two percent of our country's households with two or more children are headed by a single parent. And ninety-six percent of those are headed by the mother. I find that amazing, don't you Donna?"

Donna was not surprised. "That's a large number, George. But it could be higher. I don't see a great deal of commitment these days. Perhaps the schools should begin emphasizing faithfulness, teach it as though it were a worthwhile undertaking."

I caught Ann wrinkling her nose. She often did that when she disagreed with whoever was speaking. It was far more polite than verbal interrupting, which normally resulted in a lot of over-talk, quickly grew tedious, and was not good television.

Ever alert, Stephanopoulos had seen what I had seen, and gave Ann a nod with his head.

"Ann's face lit up. "I don't wish to quarrel with Donna, but wouldn't it be more profitable to spend our energy rediscovering our lost values? How about the old-fashioned virtue of personal responsibility? I fear that is the prime reason marriages flounder so easily today. Spouses blame each other when something goes wrong, then they put in a call to their attorney."

Donna jumped in with excellent timing, It was seamless, as if she hadn't interrupted. "How can you be so heartless, Ann?"

Stephanopoulos gave his cameraman a glance. The morning show was off to a fast start.

"It's time to leave, Jack. We shouldn't be late for church."

I hadn't heard Adrienne's footsteps on the stairs, but there she was. Dressed in gray. Standing less than three feet away, she looked quite fetching. I didn't move, simply lay there wishing.

"Jack, you need to get off the floor if we're to be on time."

She was correct, and I made my way upright. This morning I would be attending the Amazing Grace Chapel for two weeks in a row, and I was dawdling. Was it possible I was sensing remorse? By my count it had been three years since I'd gone to Holy Mass, and I felt adrift, cut loose from my moorings.

Practically speaking, my going to the Amazing Grace would pay dividends. I could keep Adrienne happy. Soon the house in Beau Arbre would be complete and she would move. Once there she would look back, recall that we had gotten along well in our Terrace Avenue home. Was it absurd to hold onto the hope that one day she might return?

My going to this chapel was temporary. It could never be more than a lily pad I would one day jump from. I was in no hurry. There would be time enough later to deal sensibly with my spiritual wanderings. My plan was to be patient, wait out my present troubles before rethinking my loss of faith. When the time was right, I would take an honest look and decide whether God had abandoned me or I had abandoned him.

Adrienne had been waiting patiently, standing in her casual way, looking sumptuous in her cashmere dress, a strand of pearls lying near her breasts.

I stood and smiled. "Let's go see what John Keats has to say."

Once again Keats was dressed as a sailor in blue pants and turtleneck sweater. The chapel was less than half full, a sparse crowd compared to last Sunday. Quite a few men had chosen not to attend. Those who were shortsighted might lay the blame squarely at the feet of Keats and his liberal leanings. I thought the cause was the cold front which had moved in. Cold air and clear skies were perfect for duck hunting. No doubt many of my friends had chosen to run over to Pecan Island. This morning they would have enjoyed a breakfast of shrimp and grits with boudin sausage on the side and arrived at their duck blinds in time to see the sun rise over the marsh. The mallards and teals would be flying, and the shooting would begin.

I loved the Louisiana wetlands and the company of such men, but this morning I had other fish to fry. I was engaged in a pretense, playing out a truce with Adrienne.

John Keats was standing at the lectern, quietly waiting for the murmuring to fade. Then he began. "From the book of Lamentations 4:17: 'Our eyes failed, ever watching vainly for help. In our watching we watched for a nation which could not save.'" He paused as if allowing a moment of reflection. "These are the words of a Jewish lament written long ago. Do they have meaning for us today? Do we, in this time of woes, look to political leaders to save us? If we do, dear friends, we look in vain. Government can never deliver us. Psalms 146:3 warns against putting your trust in the princes of this world. It is the foolish who make idols out of them. Only the Almighty God can save."

From several rows behind me a man cried out, "Amen to that!"

Keats smiled. "I hear an Amen. Do I hear another?"

There was an answering chorus, but it was mild, and Keats moved on. "The government is a creature of our own making. Why are you so quick to bow before it? Is it a fulfillment of prophecy? Did not the Book of Revelations foretell that in the last days man would create an idol with his own hands, then bow in worship?" All about me heads were nodding and why not? There was truth to what he said.

Keats's voice softened as if he were consoling a friend. "Compassion, dear friends. We are a people forever ready to give someone a second chance. We are a people willing to accept an apology when offered. We're a puffed-up people with limitless compassion, for we see ourselves as god-like. We see ourselves as the compassionate generation and we are full of pride because of it. But take care. It is all hogwash. It is the Great Deception, for we live in exile, a place where good and bad coexist."

My mind began to drift to Connor and Alfred Pohl. Pohl had shown no compassion for Scot. He viewed him as an object, something from which to make a profit. And what of Connor? What if he had viewed Pohl as merely another flawed human being, a man who had gone off the track but could be set right again if given a second chance? If we were all in need of conversion, wasn't it then possible that all could be converted?

And what of Scot? Would he one day become angry with his father for forsaking him by killing Pohl? If so, could he heal himself without learning the power of compassion? For me such thoughts evolved into a mystery with no exit. Weary of such ruminations, I once again began listening to the voice of John Keats.

"A false compassion is now being preached from the pulpits of some churches. They will point you to John 3:17. God did not send his son into the world to judge the world, but that the world might be saved. Have we been mistaken all these years? We were taught and believed Jesus Christ is to judge each of us. That he will hold us accountable for the manner in which we live. Reward the good and punish the evil. False shepherds would have you believe we have been fools…but I admonish you to ignore these heretics. Keep to the narrow way. They that preach the wide road to heaven are themselves doomed."

Once more my thoughts drifted. Keats was speaking of matters that could only be grasped at. He had a more immediate problem than the saving of souls. He had chosen a difficult city to do business in. Baton Rouge was home to Jimmy Swaggart, an entrepreneurial man of the cloth. It would be a hard climb to compete, but Keats was hard-driving and with luck could pull it off.

He held aloft a three-ring binder. "Friends of the Amazing Grace Chapel, I ask you to come forward to offer your prayers and pledges. A pledge in writing is a sign of strong faith, a commitment to God. Your faith will be preserved in this book of pledges. Let us lift our hearts to God and begin."

I smiled at Adrienne, believing a show of goodwill was the intelligent thing to do. I said, "I'll wait on the law school steps."

She gave me her determined look. "All right. But I'm going to sign the pledge Mr. and Mrs."

"Good." I headed out. She was a purposeful woman, bent on traipsing down a yellow brick road of her own making. It was becoming hard to tag along.

Outside I stood waiting for Adrienne on the thirteenth step of the law school. It was the same step I had waited on before my first exam, testing my luck, wondering if it had been used up in the Sea of Okhotsk. Across the way stood the university tower clock which looked down on the LSU parade grounds. As college boys we marched here on Tuesdays, stepping out to the strains of martial music that filled the air, proudly passing in review, dreaming of performing magic in airplanes high above the earth.

"There you are, Jack." Adrienne had found me none too soon. I was better off living in the present than remembering the past. She gave me a kiss on the cheek. "I feel like a drive. Let's go home by the lakes. It'll give us a chance to enjoy the scenery."

"Good idea. I always enjoy driving by Huey's house. He was a man before his time."

In the 1930s, mansions began popping up on the winding roads that ran beside the two lakes. The university was undergoing a building program, and there was plenty of money from the legislature for the politicians as well as the school. Later, men went to prison, but the homes remained and were handsome to look at. Huey Long was different. He'd used his own money when he built his mansion on a peninsula that jutted into one of the lakes. Huey had a good eye for land, and he also had an eye on becoming president. The country was in a serious depression, so Roosevelt promised the voters he would make sure they would have a chicken in every pot. Huey went him one better. He guaranteed he was going to make every man a king. To prove he meant what he said, he wrote a song, recorded it with him playing the piano, and put it up for sale.

"I wonder, Adrienne, what would've happened if Huey hadn't been shot and killed by Doctor Weiss. No one can say if he could've won the presidency, but it would've made us proud to be the first country where every man was a king."

Adrienne took a package of Virginia Slims from her purse and lit one. I was surprised she had taken to cigarettes but said nothing. She was not a lady who would keep at it.

"I spoke with Walter Gladden after church," she said. "He informed me that the trial begins tomorrow."

So that was it. The kiss on the cheek, then the request for a scenic drive home. All done to give her a chance to express disappointment in a space I couldn't run from.

"That's true. Jury selection was last week. It will begin for real on Monday."

"Good Lord, Jack. Fuller will never take you back now." She began searching for an ash tray but finding none, rolled down her window. "I can't believe you're doing this to us." She fell silent, pursed her lips, then started up again. "You're totally irresponsible." She tossed the cigarette from the car. "Smoking is nasty and makes everything smell."

I made no reply. I didn't doubt what she'd said about cigarettes was her way of describing how she currently felt about me. I was happy to think I would never again work for Fuller, but it had driven her to buy a package of Virginia Slims. She sat quietly, staring out the window, and I was grateful we weren't on the main road. I turned the Mustang into the narrow alleyways, which during weekdays were used by delivery vans and garbage trucks. On a Sunday, they would be untraveled and a quicker way home.

24

It wasn't until we were within sight of our house that she spoke again. "Jack, there's a strange car in our driveway."

I was surprised as well. Who was the owner of the scarred Toyota Corolla parked next to Adrienne's Lexus? It was not uncommon in trials surrounded by publicity for strangers to come forward at the last moment with information they thought might help. Had someone come to my aid? I could see no one in the Toyota, no one waiting patiently on the steps of the front porch. I looked at Adrienne. "Did we lock the house?"

"Yes, at least I think so."

Our back yard was screened by azalea bushes. If the two of us were quiet, we could use them for cover to ferret out whoever was waiting for us. We worked our way along, stopping whenever there was a small opening to peer through the leaves. We were moving slowly, had worked our way at least halfway before I spotted a woman sitting peacefully atop our bricked barbecue pit, her legs stretched out and her feet bouncing against the bricks. Mary Beth Padget.

Adrienne whispered, "Do you know her?"

There was now no need for stealth, and yet I whispered. "It's Connor's wife."

"What on earth?"

Realizing I had been in a crouch, I stood erect. "I imagine she's come to talk about Connor. Would you like to meet her?"

Adrienne gave me a look. "I most certainly intend to be introduced to any woman sitting on my barbecue pit."

I walked into the open and waited for Mary Beth to look my way. "Hi, have you been waiting long?"

Plastic drinking cup in hand, she dropped to her feet on the flagstone with one quick motion and smiled. "Hope you don't mind my coming here like this." She lifted her cup slightly, clearly at ease. "I don't think I've ever met your wife, Jack."

"Mary Beth, this is Adrienne. Adrienne…Mary Beth."

Adrienne offered her hand. "So very nice to meet you. Jack and I have just come from church."

"But of course. The way you're dressed." She ignored the edge in Adrienne's tone, but I was taking no chances.

Gently I reached for Adrienne's elbow. "Why don't you make the three of us coffee?"

Her good manners returned. "Glad you dropped by, Mary Beth. You two will want your privacy. I'll leave the coffee ready in the kitchen. I'll be upstairs."

Mary Beth resumed her perch. "I've come to find out what you think of me, Jack. Do you find that odd?"

"Not really. We've been friends for a long time."

"Be honest. You think I screwed up."

I saw no reason to respond. She would have to answer that for herself.

She sipped from her cup. "Oh, and of course there's Connor. As far as he's concerned, I've ruined everyone's life."

"It would be hard for him to see things any other way."

She nodded, looked me in the eye, then gazed past me. "My son barely speaks. That's the worst part. I worry he'll grow up and hate me."

I wanted to comfort her but was at a loss. Finally, I managed to say, "Scot's upset. That's natural."

She glanced away. "You haven't told me everything's going to be all right. I respect you for that."

Her speech was slurred. I didn't doubt she had been drinking before she arrived. I felt like a drink myself. But this was not the time for such things; she had come here to talk, and I should listen.

She began bouncing her feet, looking at them as she talked. "Connor and I weren't much of a success. There was never enough money. I went to work to pay for Scot's karate lessons. I wanted him to learn he could be good at something."

I began to search for a way out. The closest the three of us had ever been was in high school. The memories of those days were strong, remained like echoes.

"Do you recall the lines of the *Rubaiyat*, Mary Beth? We were seniors. Our English teacher insisted we discover Omar Khayyam. 'The Moving Finger writes; and, having writ, moves on: nor all thy Piety nor Wit shall lure it back to cancel half a line, Nor all thy Tears wash out a Word of it.'"

Some of the sadness disappeared from her face, chased away by a happier time. "Connor so loved memorizing. He was the best of the three of us."

"He was good at it, wasn't he?"

She laughed. "He was such a showoff about it. I loved him for it."

"Remember the year the three of us took French?"

She laughed. "Who could forget Mr. Pascal? Such a sweet man. He was a true Frenchmen, and his English was terrible."

"Pascal had us sing 'La Marseillaise' at the start of each class. Connor was the first to be able to do it from memory."

She lowered her face, and a tear formed in her eyes. "He still remembers the words. After all these years..."

Back in those days, it was easy to impress. "Connor had a knack for memorizing," I said.

"Almost a year ago, Connor and I went to the Dollar Movie near the campus to see *Casablanca*. There was that great scene when the French patriot confronts the Nazi Colonel in the bar, and everyone stands and sings the 'Marseillaise' to show whose side they're on. Connor stood up and sang along, and the people in the theatre applauded. I was embarrassed. I should've been proud of him." She reached into a pocket for a Kleenex. "I don't want to think of him in prison. You know that, don't you?"

"I'm doing what I can." My thoughts drifted to Adrienne, of her situated comfortably upstairs dreaming of life in Beau Arbre, of the coffee set aside for Mary Beth and me, which would never be drunk. The Persian poet who had authored the *Rubaiyat* had written of regret but had given no advice on how to live with it. I studied Mary Beth. Offering false hope would be no more than sending her on a fool's errand. "He'll probably spend some time in prison. You'll need to plan for that."

She jumped from her perch, a brave smile on her face. "I should be leaving. I have to create a new life for myself and my son. Will you be a gentleman and walk me to the car?"

***

It was late in the evening when I made my way to my alcove room. After Mary Beth had gone, Adrienne and I ordered Chinese and put our differences aside. Quite by accident we had discovered a TV channel showing horseracing at the Fairgrounds. Not so long ago we had been there, watched horses with names like Diplomat Way and Orleans Doge race against each other, their performance full of the run. From our table beside the window in the clubhouse, we always ordered our favorite: turtle soup and wedge salads topped with Roquefort. Now she was upstairs, either reading or sleeping, I knew not which, and I was at my desk.

It was not much of a desk, more of a writing table with a single drawer. Even so, I had done good work here for I needed only a yellow legal pad and a ballpoint pen. This evening it was my intention to outline the closing arguments to Connor's jury.

Benton would be first to speak. He was a no-nonsense man, and he would attack straight away. He was an enforcer, a law-and-order man. Administering justice was his purview, not Connor's. He would view Connor as a vigilante and would push that view until the jury was convinced Connor was a dangerous man.

I disagreed. Connor was a man who didn't trust the justice system that Benton thought so highly of. In Connor's world, criminals were often set free on technicalities. Alfred Pohl was proof of that. I had little doubt he'd been guilty as charged in Arizona, and yet the law had set him free. With his freedom he had traveled to our city and kidnapped an eleven-year-old boy.

I paused then began writing again. Connor would have to be humanized. He was no criminal. It was Alfred Pohl who was the criminal. Pohl was the one bereft of decency, a man who preyed on the innocent. Connor had done nothing more than a great many fathers would do.

I stopped writing, traced the word "justify" carefully on my notepad and underlined it. I had found an idea for my closing argument one morning as I was drinking coffee and reading *The Advocate*. It was a perfect story to use at the trial. It was tucked away in my briefcase, and I was confident it was just what I needed to convince the jury.

25

I went by the jail to see Connor. He was stoic. Said he was ready. I warned him to be careful about Benton. "He's an excellent lawyer, Connor, and he's going to attack you. Don't let him make you angry. Focus on that. Don't get mad no matter what he says, and it's always best to just be honest. Don't worry too much what you say as long as you're honest. But don't say you were jealous of Pohl if you can avoid it—and don't say more than just answering his questions when you can."

"I'm ready, Jack. Whatever it brings down on me, I'm ready. Glad you warned me about the anger. That's a good thing to remember. I'll do my best."

***

As I walked up the St. Joseph's Cathedral steps I fondly remembered better times coming here as a teenager. The smell of incense that had over the years soaked into the rafters high above seemed especially redolent. It was Monday and the start of Connor's trial in earnest. The calling of witnesses, the putting on of evidence. Secretly I wished it were Ash Wednesday. Connor would have had a better chance. A priest could have been called, come to the jail to mark his forehead with ashes as a sign to jurors he was penitent.

The young priest offering the Mass prayed the liturgy with no wasted motion, and by eight thirty-five, I was pulling my Mustang from the curb and headed for the courthouse. The trial didn't begin until nine-thirty, and I still had time to spare. Time to consider the jury and settle on one or two who might sympathize with Connor. It would take only one or two.

I particularly liked Reverend Isaiah Johnston and suspected my chances with him were between fair and good. When called for voir dire questioning, he had taken his time walking to the witness box, looking neither left nor right at the people watching him. He was a man who would ignore the opinions of others and rely on his own.

Benton had asked if he believed in the Old Testament admonishment of "an eye for an eye" as right and just. His sure-footed manner of answering appealed to me. He had smoothed down his coat jacket, held his chin high, and said, "I have pastored the Calvary Baptist Church for thirty-two years. I'm in good standing with the Christ and take Him at his word. He said that forgiveness and love were the surest path to heaven."

Benton asked again, attempting to clarify, "Is this forgiveness you speak of unlimited and without consequences? And this love you speak of—does it encompass punishing the criminal or not?"

The Reverend was quick to answer, "The Bible tells us to render unto Caesar. The State of Louisiana requires me to remain fair and impartial. I can do that."

Benton asked no more questions, and Isaiah Johnston became a member of the jury. He was the best I could hope for. He respected the law and knew his Bible.

Cecil Botts was a juror cut from different cloth. He was a man of science with his doctorate from the University of Michigan and worked for Dow Chemical. He was more to Benton's liking than mine. He was a person of accomplishment and probably held to the notion that man was master of his own fate. Suspicious he had little concern for human folly, I questioned him closely, doing what I could to eliminate him from the jury. Botts stated he was capable of listening to the evidence, able to push aside any opinion he might have formed as to Connor's guilt. He specifically promised he would disregard what he had seen on television on his way to reaching a fair and impartial verdict. The judge saw no reason to disqualify him, and the judge was right. With him on the jury, Connor had suffered a setback.

I pulled into the parking lot and gave Mrs. Couvillion a wave. She was always here, on top of her daily business, and continually happy to have bought a lot so handy to the courthouse. She reminded me a bit of Judy Bradford. I had high hopes for Judy to identify with Connor. She'd lost her job with the Baton Rouge Port Authority over a year ago and turned herself into a long-haul driver of semi-trailers. During voir dire questioning she recounted how the loss of her job had been a blessing. She was happier being independent, loved the freedom that comes with traveling the open road. I admired her, for she was just the sort who might sympathize with Connor. She had experienced a second chance, had seen firsthand the good that could come from it.

Doubt was easy to come by at the beginning of any trial, and I felt the tug of it as I left the Mustang and began my walk to the courthouse. That's when I saw the women. More than a dozen, walking back and forth on the courthouse steps with placards: Free Connor Now, Scot Needs His Father, even Go Get 'Em Jack.

I gave a wave and meant it. These women clearly believed in what I was doing, and I would do my best to do the same.

***

"Oyez, Oyez, Oyez," the bailiff cried out, "The Criminal Court in and for the Nineteenth Judicial District in and for the State of Louisiana is now in session, the Honorable Judge Frank LeBlanc presiding. The courtroom will now be in order."

Judge LeBlanc entered with a stride, took his seat, and gave a rap with his gavel. He was a seasoned veteran, senior judge of the district, and brooked no nonsense from attorneys. With a quick word to Benton, he set Connor's fate in motion. "Does the district attorney wish to make an opening statement? If so, you may proceed."

Benton rose and made his way toward the jury box. "Good morning, ladies and gentlemen. This morning we begin our search for justice. My duty is quite simple. As your attorney, I am to treat everyone equally under the law." He unbuttoned his jacket. "I have never seen this as a difficult task. All that's required is to gather evidence of wrongdoing and present it before twelve fair-minded people such as yourselves."

He turned, gestured toward Connor. "On a Monday evening the defendant attempted to take the life of Alfred Pohl. With full premeditation he shot Pohl down. Pohl later died from his wound, and Mr. Padget had his way." He moved to the evidence table, lifted from it a pistol, then dropped it. The loud bang of the pistol striking the table made the shooting more real. "A single bullet was all that was necessary. One brief act of cruelty."

Benton moved away from the table and took a step or two toward Connor. "Let us have a look at Mr. Padget. He's well-shaven, has had his hair cut recently, and is turned out in a sincere looking blue suit. Psychologists tell us that people respond to blue in a positive way. Blue is known to symbolize honesty, loyalty, and of course sincerity. Traits we all admire." Benton paused to look at me. "We attorneys are interested in such things. It's a help to us in our business because we are in the business of influencing jurors. Mr. Carney has done what he can to have Connor appear before you as an ordinary man." Benton shrugged.

"But Mr. Padget is no ordinary man. He is a man of pretense. The State of Louisiana will show you a man dressed in khaki pants and purple windbreaker. The windbreaker was not worn that night to protect against the chill but to conceal the thirty-two caliber pistol he would use to shoot Alfred Pohl. I can show you all these things because a camera crew from WAFB recorded the shooting. There will be no need for you to weigh the testimony of eyewitnesses. You'll see the shooting as it happened. Ladies and gentlemen, you will see a premeditated criminal act, carefully planned and executed."

Benton slowly buttoned his jacket. "I'm going to ask you to sentence Connor Padget to the state penitentiary at Angola for the rest of his life. It will be but simple justice."

Judge LeBlanc waited for Benton to reach the prosecutor's table before he spoke. "Mr. Carney, do you wish to make an opening statement?"

I rose. "I do, Your Honor." For a moment I stood behind Connor, my hand carefully resting on his left shoulder for the jury to see. I was waiting for the words of Benton to fade. They turned their attention my way, and I walked toward them.

"Good morning." I searched their faces for response. Some of the jurors' lips moved in reply while others reacted with half a smile. I knew it was a small thing, but I saw it as a good beginning. My intention was to make friends of them as best I could.

To appear casual, I tugged at my left ear. "Connor Padget and I have been friends since high school. During his freshman year at the university, he married Mary Beth and left LSU to take a job as a mail carrier for the post office. His wife was pregnant, and he needed to support a family."

I stopped talking, taking time to look at Benton. "The district attorney is a successful man, a man with many suits in his closet. Connor has none, so I bought the blue suit he's wearing, and I'm sure you don't mind that I did." Looks of understanding appeared, and I moved on. "What of the matter of legal representation? Connor has no money to hire a private attorney. Yes, he could have been assigned a public defender and, make no mistake, they are good lawyers, but they're always underpaid and overworked. My conscience was troubled, so I took on the job. I also initiated the Connor Fund to solicit contributions to provide for the needs of his family. The money to buy his suit and provide him with a haircut have come from that fund. As for my fee, my time and effort are without charge. I am but a friend of the family." I took time to look each juror in the eye.

"Let's move on." I walked to the evidence table and held aloft the videotape from Channel Nine. "The District Attorney would have you sentence Connor Padget to live out the rest of his life in prison because of a piece of tape enclosed in a plastic case. How has our humanity become so bastardized? When you watch this tape, you'll see what happened, but what you will not see..." I set the tape cassette back on the table. "What you will not see is why it happened. Connor Padget is a decent man, a family man. Husband to Mary Beth and father to his son, Scot. He is no more a criminal than any of you. The dead man is the criminal, and I intend to prove that."

I stood still, facing the jury. "You who sit in judgment are entitled to an explanation. He will take the stand and you will hear his reasons for his actions. Judge him then." I looked along the row until I found Reverend Johnston. "I can promise you but one thing. When this trial comes to its end, your sympathies will lie with Connor, not with Pohl." I turned toward the judge. "Thank you, Your Honor." I then looked at each juror, searching for those who would look me in the eye. "Thank you for your time."

Judge LeBlanc gave a tap with his gavel. "The prosecution may call its first witness."

Benton gave the yellow pencil he'd been fiddling with a final bounce. "The State calls Dr. Corey Townsend."

Townsend was a man come down from cattle ranching stock and walked with the gait of someone accustomed to crossing open pastures. The family had once owned land in St. Francisville, a small village just north of Baton Rouge. Tending cows had not interested the heirs, and the land had been sold. Corey Townsend was no longer a rancher but was the coroner for East Baton Rouge Parish. One might suspect his ruddy complexion and roughhewn look was an offshoot of his cowboy days, but they would be mistaken. He spent his afternoons now sitting in the sun beside the finish line at the Fairgrounds racetrack in New Orleans.

Seated in the witness chair, he gave the judge a nod and waited for Benton.

"Would you state your name and occupation?"

"Doctor Corey Townsend. Coroner for East Baton Rouge Parish."

"How long have you been coroner?"

"Eleven years, going on twelve."

"Did you perform an autopsy on Alfred Pohl?"

"I did." Townsend looked down. "I have my notes right here." He studied them, then glanced up. "I found Mr. Pohl to have been a white male with severe complications resulting from a gunshot wound. He was approximately twenty-seven years of age, weighed one hundred eighty-seven pounds, was six feet one inch tall with no visible scars. There was a single tattoo in the shape of a samurai sword on his upper chest."

He took a sip of water from a glass set out on the table beside him. "I found the cause of death to be an acute case of septic shock. I concluded that he had suffered a bullet wound several days prior to death—the bullet entered his shoulder, penetrated the lung, then passed through the colon and was embedded in his buttocks. A blood infection developed which led to clotting. This caused the kidney to fail, which resulted in a drop of blood pressure that we refer to as septic shock."

Townsend looked up at the ceiling. "Mr. Pohl need not have died from the bullet wound. All in all, I would say Mr. Pohl was a very unlucky man."

Benton nodded. "Did you examine the bullet wound?"

"I did. The size of the entry wound was such that it could have only been caused by a small caliber bullet."

Benton reached for a plastic bag on the evidence table and handed it to the witness. "I ask you to examine this bullet."

Townsend rolled the bullet in his hand, giving it a careful look before holding it for the jury to see. "This bullet killed Alfred Pohl. It's the bullet that was removed from Pohl's body by the surgeon on duty in the emergency room of Our Lady of the Lake Hospital."

Benton turned toward the judge. "Your Honor, if the defendant has no objection, I move to enter this item in evidence and have it marked State's Exhibit One."

Judge LeBlanc glanced my way out of courtesy, but I made no move to object, and the matter was over. The judge looked to his clerk. "The state's exhibit shall be so marked."

"I have no further questions, Your Honor," Benton said.

"Do you wish to cross-examine, Mr. Carney?"

"I do, Your Honor." I stood to face the witness. "During your testimony you referred to Pohl as being unlucky. What did you mean?"

"A wound like that would not normally result in death."

"Are you saying there was some intervening cause, separate and distinct from the internal damage caused by the bullet?"

"I am. In all probability there was some negligence in his treatment while in the hospital that led to his death."

"Thank you, Doctor Townsend." I glanced to the jury box. Judy Bradford's face had a sober look, and Cecil Botts was taking notes. Connor wasn't off the hook, but it was not his bullet alone that had killed Pohl.

Benton called Joe Reed, Channel Nine's breaking news reporter. Reed was one of those people you took note of. Tall with nice shoulders, he carried himself in a cheerful manner and knew his business. He was no sham reporter standing in front of a bank or convenience store that had been robbed eight hours before reporting as though it had happened only moments ago. He was an adventurer who chose the stories he covered, and when Joe Reed appeared on the screen, you knew you would get your money's worth.

Benton stood quietly, waited for Reed to take his seat and give his genial on-air smile. "Mr. Reed, I'm certain all of us in the courtroom recognize you, but please state your name and occupation for the record."

"Joe Reed, associate producer for WAFB's evening news. I also carry out all of the station's helicopter assignments."

I studied the jurors as he spoke. It was clear to see they liked him as much as I did. He would be a good witness for Benton, giving a fine edge to the viewing of the tape as he narrated the murder of Alfred Pohl.

Benton moved in close to the witness. "You have won several Louisiana journalists awards. Is that correct?"

"I've been very fortunate in that respect."

"You covered the attempted escape of two prisoners from Angola. You became quite famous for that story."

"I was given the Louisiana Broadcasters Award for Breaking News that year. It's kind of you to mention it."

"As I recall, you were presented with the keys to the city in a ceremony on the steps of the Municipal Building."

"Mayor Carr and the City Council wanted to highlight the good work journalists do for the community."

Benton raised his voice. "How could anyone forget? You, leaning from the open door of the chopper, dropping flares into the woods where you had spotted the convicts as darkness was falling."

Reed nodded modestly. "I believe the state police helicopter had experienced a mechanical problem and was late arriving."

Benton kept at it. "If the convicts had made it to the river they might well have gotten away."

Reed smiled. "I was in the right place at the right time. It's what news people try to do."

"You were also in the right place the evening of the shooting at the airport."

Reed nodded. "It turned out that way." He took a long look at the jury. "One of my sources in the sheriff's department informed me deputies would be bringing in someone who'd kidnapped a young boy. I thought it important to be there. Channel Nine is committed to focusing attention on the dangers confronting our children."

"Did your cameraman record the shooting of Mr. Pohl?"

"My cameraman was filming from the moment Pohl and the deputies entered the lobby. The camera was rolling when the shot was fired."

"Did you have a clear view of the man who did the shooting?"

"He's the man sitting beside Jack Carney." He pointed to Connor.

Benton motioned to a sheriff's deputy standing against the wall. "If it please the court, I will now have the deputy bring into the courtroom a television and ask the court's permission to play the videotape under discussion."

Judge LeBlanc nodded. "Do you have any objections, Mr. Carney?" I shook my head.

THE TRIAL OF CONNOR PADGET

The door to the courtroom opened, and a deputy rolled in a large-screen television. When it was centered for all to see, Benton slipped in the cassette. "Lights, please."

The screen lit up with a clear view of the airport lobby. Pohl appeared, walking between two deputies as though nothing important was about to happen to him. I followed him with my eyes, taking notice of the careless manner he had, and waited for the sound of the gun.

The tape played to its end, and the shooting was over, but Benton was not done. "Ladies and gentlemen, one more time." The tape began its roll, except this time it stopped just as Pohl drew close to Connor. "I would call the jury's attention to the face of the defendant."

I too studied Connor's face at the moment he raised his weapon. It was not the Connor I knew.

Only when the lights were turned back on did Benton move away from the television.

Judge LeBlanc broke the silence. "Do you wish to cross-examine, Mr. Carney?"

I looked Benton's way. His leaving the television for the jury to stare at as a reminder of what they had seen was a lawyer's trick. "I have a few questions, Your Honor. Before I begin, may I ask that the television be removed from the courtroom?"

"It is so ordered."

When the television was gone, I began. "Good afternoon, Mr. Reed, I enjoy your work."

He nodded. "Thank you."

I walked to where the television had been and gestured toward Connor. "Do you know the defendant?"

"I know who he is."

"Do you know if he's married or single?"

"It's my understanding he's married."

"Do you know if he has children?"

"I've been told he is the father of the boy Mr. Pohl allegedly kidnapped."

"Did you do any research on Connor after this incident?"

"Yes, I needed to for follow-up stories."

"He has lived, worked, and raised a family in this area all his life. Did you find any criminal record?"

"No."

"Any news stories about him?"

"Not until mine."

"So up to then, just a normal family man. What about yourself, Mr. Reed. Are you married?"

"I'm single."

"You testified that you were particularly interested in stories which focused on the vulnerability of children. Is that so?"

Turning towards the jury, he spoke in his on-air voice, "I have covered the killings of children at their schools, have seen their blood in hallways. It's a shocking experience." He paused. "I covered the story of the priest at Saint Margaret Mary who molested children. These things affect a person."

He fell silent, and I waited for the mood he had set to take hold. Slowly I moved to the evidence table and reached for Connor's pistol. "This weapon belonged to the defendant. It was used in the shooting at the airport."

"Yes, I was there."

It was a good sign for Reed to break in. He was speaking earnestly of the need to protect our children. That could only help Connor. "Mr. Reed, you're a thoughtful man. Have you ever wondered what the defendant's motive for the shooting might have been?"

"I've heard rumors. As a journalist I'm not comfortable dealing in conjecture."

"Pohl was arrested, charged with kidnapping. You were aware of that. That's the reason you were at the airport, wasn't it?"

"Yes."

I edged closer, trying to gauge what had happened. Reed was a man of composure, accustomed to stress, but in a small way he had given in. "If you had a son who was sexually abused and you knew who did it, what would you do? Could you become so enraged you would kill such a man?"

"Objection, Your Honor!" Behind me, Benton leaped to his feet and left the counsel table to stand near me. "This is outrageous, Your Honor. Mr. Pohl is not on trial. The man who murdered him is."

Judge LeBlanc's eyes narrowed, but his face showed no signs of agitation. "Objection sustained. Mr. Carney, I suggest you move on to a different line of questioning."

"Thank you, Your Honor. I have no further questions." I'd taken my gamble. Joe Reed's concern for children had given me a chance to plant the seed of molestation, and the possibility of such having happened was now fixed in the minds of the jurors. Benton's outburst had but added to the impact and might even be reminiscent of a cover-up.

Judge LeBlanc watched Reed leave the courtroom before making a point of looking at his watch. "This trial is now in recess. Court will resume at 1:30." As the jurors began filing out, Judge LeBlanc addressed Benton and me. "Mr. Jones, it's my understanding you plan to call three witnesses this afternoon."

"Yes, Your Honor. The ballistics expert who will testify that the bullet removed from Pohl was fired from Padget's thirty-two, and the deputies who were escorting Pohl."

"I'll anticipate a quiet afternoon." The judge tugged at the sleeves of his robe. "And tomorrow?"

"The state will call Mary Beth Padget, wife of the accused."

The judge stood. "Gentlemen, let's go to lunch."

26

It was six-thirty in the evening and Adrienne was moving about the kitchen preparing dinner. I sat in the nook of our breakfast room with a clear view of her. She was in her tennis dress, fresh from her Wednesday game at the club, and the dress lay softly against her hips.

The shape of her rounded figure had brought me comfort over the years. This evening I no longer cared. Was it love that stirred, and without it did attraction flatten? She was lovely to look at, but there was an emptiness to it now. I no longer saw her as Adrienne. Now she was too much like the others who fancied being admired.

I watched her have a look at the Cornish hens roasting in the oven. She smiled in satisfaction. "Thomas expects it to rain all week. He said we were lucky to get the roof up on the house when we did."

I saw no point in conversation about a house I wanted no part of. And yet I wasn't looking for trouble, so I answered with a grunt.

She slid a batch of asparagus onto a skillet. "Thomas says this year's rainy season has been the worst in years. And if anyone knows, it's him. He keeps up with each day's rainfall, keeps the figures in a special blue book he carries."

"Hmm. Piggott is a man full of information, and I'm growing tired of it."

She looked at me. "You know I don't like it when you talk that way." She turned to the range and checked the wild rice boiling in a pot of water. "You appreciate nice things. Admit it."

"I want to live simply, Adrienne. The people who live in Beau Arbre don't."

"Piggott thinks it's possible you resent my money. Is that it?"

I didn't doubt Piggott had said such a thing. Wealthy people tended to believe others envied them. "I don't resent your money. I resent you wasting it on a house you have no need of."

She kept at her cooking as if nothing I said mattered. She slid the asparagus onto a serving plate. Out came the Cornish hens roasted and browned, deftly arranged next to the asparagus. Wealth hollowed people out. Adrienne was becoming one of them. I needed a drink. I passed behind her, took my bottle of Russian vodka from the freezer, and with shot glass in hand, returned.

Adrienne began ladling out the wild rice. "The house is almost built. I'm going to live there. You can't stop me."

"I could sue for abandonment."

"That isn't funny."

"No, it isn't…but it's the law. You can't make me move from this house. You can leave—but I can sue you for abandoning me, which is what you're up to."

"You wouldn't do that, Jack. It's not your style."

"No, I wouldn't. But it should make you realize what you're doing."

I eyed the platter of food Adrienne had arranged so neatly. Suddenly I wanted none of it. "It's been a long day. I'm afraid I don't have much of an appetite."

"I'll never understand why you took Connor as a client. So, don't ask me to. Oh — I forgot — Kathy called earlier today."

I stood up with the bottle and shot glass. "It's probably important. I'll call her from the study." Tucked away, I punched in Kathy's number. "Hi, you called?"

"Guess who's in town. Rebecca Wylie. She was in the courtroom today. When the trial is over, she wants an interview."

"I don't see the point."

"You're dealing with the media, Jack, that's the point. She's already spoken to Benton, and he agreed to an interview. That means you have to as well. She's going to write a magazine piece, and you can't let her readers only be exposed to Benton's perspective. You owe it to Connor."

Kathy was speaking with the authority of someone who was certain. How was it I thought she was entirely wrong? With the trial over, I'd be off to Sanibel. What did it matter to me what some reader of the words of Rebecca Wylie thought?

I played for time. "There's some truth to what you say." If I could do Kathy a favor, I would, even if it meant speaking with Rebecca Wylie at a time when my thoughts would surely be about Connor. Then an idea struck. Rebecca Wylie's magazine piece would be of no help to Connor, but that didn't mean she couldn't help him. She was a woman with connections. "I'll do the interview."

"You won't be sorry, Jack. Thank you."

I waited a moment. "Do you have Rebecca's private number? I'd like to speak to her personally."

"Sure, she'll be glad you called."

I said goodbye and dialed the number. She answered promptly, "Rebecca Wylie speaking."

"This is Jack Carney. Kathy just called, and I understand you were in the courtroom today."

"Yes, that's true. So nice of you to call. I admired the way you conducted yourself… I found it all very interesting."

"I need a favor."

"How can I be of help?"

"It concerns Alfred Pohl. I've filed a Freedom of Information Act request for any background information from the FBI. The bureaucracy is slow and unreliable, and I've gotten no answer. I was hoping you might be able to help."

"I have friends in the Bureau. You'll have what you need tomorrow if I can manage it."

"By the way, I've just spoken to Kathy. I'd be more than happy to sit for an interview."

"Wonderful. I've been commissioned to write a piece for *The New Yorker*. Your interview will be a huge help. Is there anything else?"

"You can wish me luck."

"May the luck of the Irish be with you."

I said good night, filled the shot glass, and sipped at my vodka. I'd always seen myself as one of the lucky ones, and with help from Kathy and Ms. Wylie, I didn't doubt my luck was holding. I would finish this drink, have another for luck, then work on the closing argument. It was going to be the key to this case and held any hope of winning.

27

"The State of Louisiana calls Mary Beth Padget."

I heard the tapping of heels, listened as they drew close. Mary Beth passed me, dressed in a blue skirt and tan sweater. She had tied a pale, light blue scarf around her neck.

Connor leaned against me whispering, "Here we go, Jack."

I thought it a sorry situation and a poor thing for Benton to be doing. Benton was acting in good faith. I didn't doubt that. He believed what he believed, that Connor had killed Pohl because of an affair. If that was so, then why had Connor waited until Pohl had kidnapped his son? I didn't like the idea of Mary Beth having to admit to her affair in front of Connor or to deny it and so commit perjury. The difference between Benton and me boiled down to how we looked at things. He viewed Connor and Mary Beth as strangers while I did not.

Benton began. "Would you state your name and address."

"Mary Beth Padget. I live at 2234 Horseshoe Bend Road with my son, Scot Padget."

Benton remained seated at the counsel table. "At some point your son became interested in karate, is that so?"

"Scot was small for football. He asked if he could have karate lessons."

"When the subject of these lessons first arose, were you already acquainted with Mr. Pohl?"

"Oh, no. I knew nothing about karate. I was given Pohl's name by a friend."

"Who paid for these lessons?"

"I did. With the money I was earning at Mrs. Dameron's dress shop."

"I assume you saw to it that Scot was taken to the studio and picked up when the lesson was over."

"I drove him."

"Did there come a time when you remained at the studio during the lesson?"

"Yes, I was interested in my son's progress."

"Did other parents remain at the studio during the lesson?"

"No."

"During this period of time you developed a friendship with Mr. Pohl, is that true?"

"Mr. Pohl was an easy-going man. I saw no reason not to like him."

Benton rose. "Let's turn our attention to your son. How would you describe Scot's relationship with Pohl?"

Mary Beth looked directly at Connor as she answered. "He liked Mr. Pohl a great deal. He was excited about traveling to Memphis with him."

Benton hitched his belt. "No doubt you were pleased to see your son happy."

"Of course."

Benton glanced toward the jury. "I take it you developed a sense of gratitude toward Pohl. I would think that would be a natural reaction for a mother."

"I appreciated what he was doing for my son."

Benton set out pacing. "Did this appreciation result in your rewarding Pohl with sexual favors?"

Mary Beth pulled back, as if surprised, and stared back at him. "We were friends, nothing more."

Benton turned to look at Connor. "Clearly your husband thought otherwise. Wasn't this so-called friendship the reason your husband moved from your home to live alone in an apartment?" He took a few steps toward Mary Beth. "If there was some other reason for his leaving, please tell us what it was."

She shrugged. "Connor's job at the post office didn't pay that well. I took a job thinking it would help, but he thought I was becoming too independent. That's the reason he left."

Benton reached for a sheet of paper. "Mrs. Padget, you have sworn to tell the truth. If you testify falsely, you will be committing perjury and be subject to criminal prosecution. Do you understand?"

Mary Beth answered in a deliberate way. "I don't frighten easily, Mr. Jones."

"Good. The District Attorney's Office is not in the business of frightening witnesses. We are in the business of seeing to it they testify truthfully." Benton directed his attention to Judge LeBlanc. "Your Honor, may I approach the witness?"

The judge's eyes crinkled. "If the purpose is to impeach the witness because of a prior inconsistent statement, you may."

Benton moved near Mary Beth. "You have denied any extramarital affair with Pohl. Do you stand by that statement?"

Mary Beth's chin came up. "There was no affair."

Benton flicked his wrist, popped the sheet of paper, and began reading. "My name is Mary Beth Padget. I am giving this statement freely and voluntarily under no threat nor promise of reward to Sergeant Daniels. I acknowledge that I engaged in a brief sexual affair with Alfred Pohl. I further state that it is my belief this affair was the motive for my husband, Connor Padget, shooting Alfred Pohl." Benton began rocking to-and-fro. "Tell us, Mary Beth. Were you lying when you gave that statement to my investigator or are you lying to us now?"

"I lied to your investigator, but I had my reasons."

Benton smirked. "And what was that reason?"

Mary Beth stared as if into nothingness. "My husband was convinced Pohl could have molested our son. I was certain he hadn't. I was afraid Connor would do something rash, so I told him that I had slept with Pohl. That Pohl could not possibly be interested in Scot. I told him that in the hope it would calm him down. I didn't see any harm in telling your investigator the same story I'd told Connor."

Benton shook his head. "Why continue the lie after the shooting? What you're saying doesn't make sense."

Mary Beth's voice was barely audible. "My son was kidnapped. Had been in police custody. My husband had shot someone. I was naturally quite upset and confused. Somehow it made sense to tell the same story."

I glanced at the jury. Cecil Botts was taking notes, and Judy Bradford's face was lined with sympathy.

Benton was unaffected. "Let's examine what sort of cake we are baking here, shall we? Your family is getting by, paying the bills, but not much more. You take a job to help, and your husband shows no appreciation. You meet someone you describe as something of a father figure in your son's life." Benton paused, slowly unbuttoned his jacket as if he were a man who had finally gotten to the bottom of things. "No one could blame you for having an affair."

"I had no affair." The only sound in the courtroom came from the traffic on the streets.

The silence lingered until finally Benton addressed the judge. "Your Honor, I have no more questions of this witness."

Judge LeBlanc looked to me. "Do you wish to cross-examine?"

"Yes, Your Honor." I walked toward the witness stand, stopped short of Mary Beth, and turned toward Benton. "That was quite an ordeal wasn't it?"

She glanced at the jurors. "Yes, it was."

"The district attorney has made it quite clear that he wants everyone in this courtroom to believe you had sexual relations with Alfred Pohl. He actually believes that, doesn't he?"

Benton was quick to rise. "Your Honor, I object. Please instruct Mr. Carney to stick to asking questions of the witness instead of making accusations."

Judge LeBlanc gave a tap of his gavel. "The district attorney is quite correct. Keep your observations to yourself, Mr. Carney.

I merely turned to Mary Beth. "It's time for the truth, Mrs. Padget. Did you have sex with Alfred Pohl? Yes or no?"

"Mr. Pohl was my son's karate instructor, nothing more. As far as he was concerned, I was merely Scot's mother. Sorry to disappoint the district attorney, but there was nothing sexual between us."

"But you trusted him. You liked him."

"Of course. He was employed by a school with a good reputation, and he was teaching my son something new and exciting. Tell me why I shouldn't have."

"Eventually, you bought a karate uniform for yourself. Is that true?"

"It was Scot's idea."

"Your husband claims you were taking karate lessons. Lessons for which there was no charge. Is that also true?"

"I resent what you're implying. Everything I did was innocent. Scot wanted me to have a uniform like he did, so I bought one. And I was not taking lessons. I simply stood in the back of the room and copied their movements. Scot and I wanted to have something in common."

"Let's turn our attention to Scot's tournament in Memphis. I take it you were told the tournament ended on Saturday and that Scot would return Sunday. Is that correct?"

"Yes."

"That wasn't true, was it?"

"The tournament was supposed to end on Saturday. Pohl told me they had another playoff round for Sunday, though."

"Did you speak to Scot while he was in Memphis and, if so, on how many occasions?"

"I spoke to Scot on Friday evening. I used Mr. Pohl's cell number to reach him."

"Was the conversation normal?'

"Scot had lost his match, but he didn't seem upset. He was somehow still in the tournament."

"And the next time you spoke to Scot was when?"

"I called Saturday evening, but I didn't speak to Scot. Mr. Pohl told me he'd gone to a pizza party organized by the tournament for the boys who'd won that day. I was excited to hear that Scot had won his match, and I thought no more of it."

"And that was another lie, wasn't it?"

"Yes, it was. Scot lost both his matches. We didn't discover that until we had him home."

"Let's go back to that Saturday. You could have called again that evening when Scot would have returned from the pizza party, isn't that so?"

"Perhaps I should have, but I didn't want to be one of those worrying mothers. I was under the impression the tournament was held over, and they would be home Sunday night. It wasn't until no one showed up that I called again to see what was going on."

"So you called again on Sunday night?"

"Yes, but no one answered. The call went to voicemail. The same thing happened again on Monday."

"Is that when you became concerned?"

"Of course. I called the MacMaster's people and they confirmed the tournament had ended Saturday night. They gave me contact information for Scot and his coach at Holiday Inn Express. I called the motel, and Pohl wasn't registered. That's when I knew something was wrong and called the Memphis police."

"Tell the jury what happened the following day."

"I got a phone call from the clerk at a Quik Pak in Memphis. She said my son was there, and then she put Scot on the phone."

"What happened next?"

"I told Scott to stay where he was, that I would call the police, and they would bring him home."

"And when Scot was home, did you ask him how Pohl had frightened him?"

"Yes, he said—"

Benton was on his feet. "I object, Your Honor. Anything Scot said to someone else is hearsay and inadmissible. Scot can take the stand and speak for himself."

Judge LeBlanc nodded. "Sorry, Mr. Carney, but you'll have to move on."

"Under the circumstances I have no further questions."

Judge LeBlanc gave Mary Beth a kindly look. "The witness is excused but will remain in the courtroom in case either attorney wishes to recall her."

Mary Beth walked past me, looking neither to the right nor left.

"The State of Louisiana rests its case, Your Honor," Benton said.

The judge looked at me. "Is the defense prepared to call its first witness?"

"Yes, Your Honor. The defense calls Gloria Doyle."

Gloria, dressed in a dark grey pants suit with her hair tied in a knot, took the witness seat and gave a respectful glance to the jurors.

"Please give the court your name and occupation."

"Gloria Doyle. My husband and I own the Art of Karate Studio."

"Is the studio located in the city?"

"It's on Government Street in the Goodings strip mall."

"Did you at one time employ a person by the name of Alfred Pohl?"

"Yes. He worked as one of our instructors until his death."

"Would you tell us how that employment came about?"

"In a totally normal manner. He completed an application and based on that information we hired him."

"I see. Did he furnish a place of prior employment?"

"He claimed to have been an instructor for three years at Gibson's Martial Arts in Phoenix. Gibson's is highly respected."

"And did you verify his employment at Gibson's?"

"That was the mistake we made. For some reason we didn't believe it was necessary."

"It would have taken but a phone call. And yet you didn't bother?"

"We were careless. It was a terrible mistake, but Pohl impressed us. We conducted a thorough interview, not only as to the physical but also the spiritual aspects of martial arts. Mr. Pohl was very knowledgeable."

"Did there come a time when you contacted Gibson's to verify his employment?"

"Yes, the day you appeared at our studio." She tilted her head slightly. "May I say something, Mr. Carney?"

"Of course."

"My husband and I would like everyone to know how sorry we are. We can't undo what's happened, but we did want to do something. We're donating one thousand five hundred dollars to the Connor Fund."

"That's very kind of you. Connor's family will appreciate it. Now let's return to Mr. Pohl—what did you learn when you contacted Gibson's?"

"I object, Your Honor," Benton said before the witness could answer. "The question calls for hearsay. Ms. Doyle cannot speak for Gibson's. Only Gibson's can. Mr. Carney should know that."

"Of course it's hearsay, Your Honor. I was simply attempting not to unduly delay the pace of the trial."

"Mr. Jones's objection is sustained. The witness may not answer." Judge LeBlanc tugged at the sleeve of his gown and gave a wry grin. "Now, Mr. Carney, what is this about speeding up our proceedings? I'm always in favor of that."

"Your Honor. It would have been an unreasonable burden to have an employee of Gibson's flown to Baton Rouge to testify to the uncontested fact that Pohl was never an employee at their school. I have made other arrangements. A member of Gibson's human resource department has agreed to testify by Skype as to Pohl's employment."

"I don't like your idea, Mr. Carney. I would consider that to be a burden on the Court. What other option do you have?"

"I anticipated Your Honor might be of such an opinion. I have an alternative." I reached into my briefcase. "I have here a sworn affidavit from Gibson's which states that Alfred Pohl was never an employee at their school." I handed the paper to Benton. "If you find this in order I assume you will withdraw your objection."

Benton took but a moment to study the affidavit. "I have no wish to unnecessarily prolong the trial. I withdraw my objection."

Judge LeBlanc asked, "Mr. Carney, do you have any additional evidence of this nature?"

"I do. First I would like to ask the witness a single question in order to lay a proper foundation."

"Proceed."

"Ms. Doyle, did you in my presence telephone MacMaster's World of Martial Arts and learn from them that the name listed for Scot's instructor for the Memphis tournament was Allen Parker and not Alfred Pohl?"

"Yes, I did."

"Did it surprise you that Pohl was using an alias?"

"I was shocked. I had thought so highly of him."

"Were you aware that Scot was going to participate in the Memphis tournament?"

"No, that was a surprise as well."

"And why is that?"

"Scot was a novice. He wasn't qualified for such a prestigious tournament."

I went to my counsel table, reached into my briefcase and withdrew the MacMaster invitation. "Ms. Doyle, is this the invitation you received from MacMaster's?"

"Yes, it is. You can see right away it's expensive to produce. It shows you how important a tournament it is. Scot had no business being there."

I handed her the invitation. "Would you look at the invitation and tell the jury when the tournament ended?"

"Certainly. The tournament was to end at 7:00 p.m. on Saturday."

I turned to the Judge. "I ask the bailiff to deliver these documents labeled one through four to the jurors as evidence for their personal examination. Document three is a copy of the résumé Mr. Pohl presented to the Doyle's when he was hired, and four is the invitation to the MacMaster's Tournament from Ms. Doyle's records."

The judge turned to Benton. "Do you accept these documents as evidence, Mr. Jones?"

"I do, Your Honor. I also agree they may be delivered to the jurors for their inspection."

Miss Idell bent to record the introduction of the documents into evidence, then handed them to the bailiff. Judge

LeBlanc watched carefully until the jury had all looked at the evidence presented.

I had no further questions, and Benton declined any cross-examination.

"Are you now ready, Mr. Carney, to call your next witness?"

"Yes, Your Honor. The defense calls Connor Padget."

Connor made his way up to the witness stand looking good in his blue suit. The clerk read the words of the oath while I shuffled through papers pretending to study them. I wanted the jurors to have a good look at the man who had been charged with the murder of Alfred Pohl. My hope was they would see him for what he was, the father of a young boy who had been kidnapped. A man who posed no threat to society.

Allowing the silence to settle over the courtroom, I waited for Judge LeBlanc's patience to wear thin, kept at my shuffling until I heard the tap of his gavel.

"The court doesn't wish to trouble you, Mr. Carney, but we're waiting."

"Sorry, Your Honor. Mr. Padget, how well did you know Alfred Pohl before you shot him?"

"I met him only once, the evening Mary Beth and I signed Scot up for lessons."

"Did there come a time when you resented Alfred Pohl because of his relationship with your son?"

"Scot enjoyed the lessons. How could I resent that?"

"Are you asking us to believe you felt no animosity toward Pohl?"

"I was angry, but it wasn't something I couldn't handle. Not until this Memphis trip."

Standing, I moved away from the counsel table. "Memphis changed everything, didn't it?"

Connor let out a long breath. "It did."

"Did your wife seek your permission to allow Scot to travel to Memphis—alone with a man who was not a relative, not even a friend of the family?"

Connor turned to look at the jury. "No, she didn't."

"There came a time, did it not, when Mary Beth informed you that Scot hadn't come home from the tournament when he was supposed to?"

"Yes."

"Had Pohl contacted your wife to give a reason for the delay?"

"No, she'd heard nothing from Pohl. She tried reaching him but couldn't. He wasn't answering his phone."

"But at some point, Scot did get in touch with Mary Beth?"

"That's when Scot escaped. He called his mother from Memphis."

"What happened next?"

"I called my cousin. She works for the sheriff's office. She said she would have Deputy Trotsclair get in touch with me."

"And did he?"

"Yes. He said he'd contact the Memphis police and arrange for Scot to be brought home." He turned away from the jury to look directly at Benton. "I explained that Scot had been kidnapped. Told the deputy Scot had gone there with Alfred Pohl. Deputy Trotsclair was sympathetic, told me he would see to it that Pohl was arrested and extradited."

"Do you know if your son was harmed in any way in Memphis?"

Connor's face turned grim. "I regret that part." He looked toward Benton. "I never asked him about what happened. Mary

Beth and I decided it was best not to ask anything the first evening when he came home. We thought it would be wiser to simply show him we loved him. Let him adjust to the fact that he was home. That he was safe. It was the only time I was with him. The next day I shot Pohl."

"Do you know if Scot has been examined by a physician?"

"Mary Beth and I discussed it. I wanted it; Mary Beth was against it."

I stepped toward the jury, then stopped. "You had no proof Scot had been harmed, and yet you took it upon yourself to shoot Pohl. Tell us why."

Connor spoke in a calm, measured voice. "Pohl was a stranger who came into my life. He took advantage of my wife. I accepted that and moved to an apartment. Then he went after my son. He kidnapped Scot for a reason. If not to molest him, then for what? Alfred Pohl was up to no good. He was an evil man and was evading the law. That's why I shot him."

Taking my time, I looked at each of the jurors. "There you have it. Your Honor, I have no more questions."

Benton rose, his voice cold and flat. "I'm curious, Mr. Padget. How does it feel to kill someone?"

"I object, Your Honor. The district attorney is attempting to badger the witness."

"Objection sustained."

Benton shrugged. "You did shoot and kill someone though, didn't you? Everyone in this courtroom has seen you do it."

"Yes."

"You're a troubled man, Mr. Padget. You move to an apartment because your wife is having an affair. Your son begins to look upon your wife's lover as a father figure. You're at a loss for what to do. Then some difficulty arises in Memphis, and you seize upon that as an excuse to make all your troubles go away. You, sir, have no idea what happened in Memphis, and yet you want this jury to believe you do. You, sir, lost control of your family and you are to blame, not some dead man who cannot speak for himself. You, sir, are the sole reason Alfred Pohl is dead. Isn't that so?"

Connor shook his head. "Alfred Pohl kidnapped my son. That's why I went to the airport that evening."

Benton frowned and made his way toward the witness stand. "Do you believe in the law, Mr. Padget? I ask you that because you are in a court of law and the law is all around you." Benton unbuttoned his jacket and slowly gazed about the courtroom. "The law is the solemn expression of the legislature. It is the will of the people. These twelve men and women of the jury are strangers to one another and yet they're bound together by the law, by their swearing an oath to judge you fairly based solely on the evidence presented in this courtroom. Judge LeBlanc has sworn an oath to see to it that you receive a fair trial. There are three deputy sheriffs in this courtroom to protect you and ensure order. So, I ask you again, do you believe in the law?"

Connor looked at the jury. "I was worried Pohl would get away with what he'd done to my son. I was concerned he'd get off on some technicality. Everyone knows that happens."

Benton's voice was cold. "That evening at the airport you thumbed your nose at the law, Mr. Padget. You acted as a vigilante would. Vigilantism brings anarchy, not justice. That evening you spit in the face of justice. Do you understand that, sir?"

Connor answered softly, the words barely audible. "Pohl was an intruder. I was protecting my family."

Benton walked away as Connor was speaking, was midway to the counsel table before he turned to address the judge. "I have no further questions of this witness, Your Honor."

The judge tapped his gavel. "The witness is excused." He turned to me. "Mr. Carney, how many witnesses do you have for tomorrow?"

"Only one, Your Honor – Connor's son, Scot Padget."

Judge LeBlanc nodded, brought his gavel down hard. "Court will reconvene tomorrow at 9:30 a.m."

Miss Idell gave a wave of her hand at my mentioning of Scot. Now she stood, crooking a finger at me. I made my way toward her. "Jack, you have a problem. Scot has gone missing. Lt. Trahan called from the sheriff's office. He's been unable to serve the subpoena for Scot to testify, and the mother is not cooperating."

28

I made my way out of the courthouse. Time for counting on hope had run its course. Mary Beth had hidden Scot, and Connor's trial would end with a whimper. I could do nothing. Every search needs to have a beginning, and I was without one. Mary Beth's concern for her son had turned her into an adversary.

I decided to drive to clear my head. I went back in time, thought of Harper Lee, a wise lady from Alabama who had written *To Kill a Mockingbird*. She had written of Atticus Finch, an attorney who took the search for justice among men seriously. Contrary to the wisdom of the world, Atticus had undertaken the defense of Tom Robinson. Tom had been convicted in the end which was no surprise to anyone, black or white, living in Maycomb, Alabama. Had what Atticus done been a waste? He didn't think so, and neither did I. The thought of Atticus bucking the hard wind, all the while sailing a steady course, cheered me as I drove.

Up ahead was Pendry Road which led to the River Road. I didn't hesitate and took the exit. This was as good a time as any to see what Adrienne and Thomas Piggott had been up to all these months. I slid in a George Strait CD and headed for Beau Arbre listening to George sing about reaching "Amarillo by Morning."

Twenty minutes later I spotted the brick wall that marked Beau Arbre. At its entrance was a sentry box and beside it a man dressed in British tan military khaki. He motioned me to stop and peered down at me. "If you want a tour, I'll call a realtor."

"I'm Jack Carney. My wife is building on Wisteria Lane."

He stepped smartly into the sentry box to fetch a clipboard. "Driver's license?"

He examined it, smiled, then quick as a wink affixed a Beau Arbre decal to the windshield of the Mustang. "Next time you won't have to stop. Wisteria Lane is the second street past the creek."

I pulled to the curb, now face-to-face with my wife's West Indies house. It was almost finished, looked as if it wouldn't be long before the landscaping began. Today the ground was bare except for the lumber walkways used when rain turned the ground to mud.

I entered the house, stopped in the foyer, and heard sounds of scraping. I made my way toward it, rounded a doorway, and spotted a gray-haired man hard at work on a fireplace. He had heard me, I was certain, but continued his work as though he did not take kindly to interruption.

"Hello," I called out.

He remained bent to his work, as if I hadn't spoken, and the scraping continued.

"I'm the husband. I came to look around. Okay?"

"Sure, mister. I heard you."

I moved closer. "That's a large fireplace you're working on."

"The ones upstairs are smaller."

I wandered outside and surveyed the yard, saw how it gently sloped toward an oak tree. All the lumber walkways ended a short distance from the patio except one which had been laid to the base of that tree. Piggott was not a wasteful man, so if the planks were there they served some purpose. I made my way over them and stopped when I saw a sheet of Adrienne's pink stationary nailed to the tree. It was clear to me I had stumbled upon some private business of my wife's. Closing in on the tree I read Adrienne's delicate script.

Jarreau's—2:30

With a lawyer's habit, I removed the note and folded it neatly into my wallet.

Jarreau's served boiled shrimp and crab tasty enough to attract customers from New Orleans as well as Baton Rouge. It was not unreasonable for the two of them to meet there to enjoy a meal while they discussed the progress on the house. It was the cabins for rent out back that concerned me. Jarreau's was but thirty minutes south, and I would find out for myself.

The white clapboard building that was Jarreau's stood at a bend of the river surrounded by flat farmland and was visible from a distance. Except for Adrienne's Lexus and Piggott's Mercedes, the parking lot was empty.

The large dining room was inviting, but I saw no one, so made my way to the back and the screened-in porch. It was empty as well, but it did provide a clear view of five cabins nestled among a stand of oleander bushes. I wondered which one they had chosen. I felt angry. I felt betrayed. I felt like Connor. I wanted nothing more than for the pain to be over.

Back inside I found the bar and behind it a stocky Cajun watching television. He glanced my way. "We have some nice river shrimp if you've come to eat."

"A shot of house bourbon will do." I pulled out the stool opposite him.

"Want a chaser with it? I carry a nice beer brewed in New Orleans."

"Okay."

He poured from a bottle of Jim Beam. "You from around here or just passing through?"

"Born and raised in Baton Rouge." I drank the bourbon, then sipped the beer. "Not much business this time of day is there?"

"Nope." He reached for a cloth and wiped the already clean bar. "Another?"

"That would be fine."

He refilled the shot glass. "A plate of river shrimp would go good with the rest of your beer."

The bourbon was warm and the beer cold. "I'm actually waiting for friends and am not sure about the time. I'll wait a bit yet."

I heard the sound of a door opening, then the voices of Adrienne and Piggott. The bartender heard them as well. He moved from behind the bar and headed for the dining room.

"It's your lucky day," I heard him say. "We're offering boiled river shrimp. They're hard to come by."

"Sounds delicious." Hearing Adrienne's voice caused a certain sadness. One of the things we did best together was to visit waterfront restaurants in out-of-the-way places.

"That's it then. We'll have two plates and two bottles of whatever beer you recommend," Thomas ordered with precision. It was the voice of a man in charge.

I shouldn't have come. I should have left the note nailed to the tree and gone about my business. An odd feeling as if I were an intruder enveloped me. The bartender walked past and disappeared into the kitchen. He gave me a half wink as he went by, letting me know that he was happy he'd found two people who knew the value of a catch of river shrimp. I wondered how he would react if he knew who the three of us were. I swallowed a sip of bourbon, followed that with a sip of beer, and waited for him to return.

Soon he was back at the bar and came over to see if I needed anything.

"I'll bet you have some George Strait songs on your jukebox."

"Yes, sir. Always do. We have three of his best."

"How about "Give It Away?""

"That's one of his sad songs. But we have it."

"For me today's not a happy day."

The lyrics played and I listened. Thought about the good days Adrienne and I had spent together. I listened some more and grew used to the notion that change has a way of destroying things and building hope in what will turn up next. The song had almost ended when the bartender disappeared into the kitchen. He reappeared carrying a tray with the two plates of shrimp and came near on his way to the dining room.

I stopped him, handed him a twenty and Adrienne's pink note. "Do me a favor. Tuck this under the lady's plate when you serve them. This is a message to them… I used to know those people."

I finished my bourbon, left cash for my drinks, and walked away. I was halfway through the door to the parking lot when I heard the sound of breaking glass. I hesitated for a moment, not knowing. It was possible she had simply knocked a glass over in surprise. On the other hand, she might as easily have thrown her glass at the wall. Deep inside I preferred the latter.

29

I awoke to the sound of the phone in the kitchen. "Hello."

"Jack?"

"Yes." I glanced at the clock on the wall, which showed 5:30 in the morning.

"Lieutenant Trahan. We've located Scot."

I sat up straight. "Where?"

"Across the river, south of Plaquemine."

"Can you get a subpoena over there before court opens?"

"Too much paperwork. Besides, it wouldn't do much good. Scot's at the home of a lady with connections. The minute the subpoena arrived at the clerk's office, she would know and simply move the boy."

"Who's the woman?"

"Gloria Sonnier. She and her husband have a place ten miles south of Plaquemine. The husband's offshore on a rig, so she's alone."

"How did the Sonniers get involved?"

"The wife is related in some way. You know, somebody married somebody's cousin."

"Thanks for the heads-up, Lieutenant."

I dialed Kathy. "This is Jack. I realize it's early."

"I've been trying to reach you. Did you finally check your phone?"

Her voice was pleasant, as if she came awake easily. I was all set to tell her of my plan to rescue Scot, but first things first. "You go first. What did you call about?"

"Rebecca Wylie faxed me a dossier on Alfred Pohl. She found new information that should help, mainly that he uses an alias. And he's a man with a record. For starters, Alfred Pohl is not his real name. His real name is Allen Barker. He's also used the name Adam Gardener. He has one conviction for passing counterfeit money, two charges of kidnapping but no convictions due to technicalities, and he has moved around a lot mainly in California and Arizona. Ms. Wylie was onto something. She said children were being kidnapped and sold for snuff films, remember?"

"Where in California did Pohl live?"

"Culver City, Inglewood, and Huntington Park, all within twenty miles of LA."

This was good news. Pohl was a criminal, and he'd lived near the film industry. Pohl's record was not proof certain as to why he had kidnapped Scot, but it would give the jury something to work with. Was it enough to sway Reverend Johnston or Judy Bradford? What I did know was the jury would need to look at Scot to wonder how close he had come to being murdered.

"Pohl's record is a good break for Connor. But now he needs one more. It's the reason I called."

"If I can help, I will."

"We need to rescue Scot. Mary Beth is hiding him across the river so he can't testify."

"I'm in. You know where I live."

"Lakeshore Manors?"

"Give me fifteen minutes. I'll be in the lobby."

It was a little before six o'clock when I arrived at the Lakeshore, which looked more like a hotel with its view of the lake from the grand lobby. It was a good place for a girl like Kathy to live and was but a mile from the up ramp to the Mississippi River bridge. Wrapped in a coat against the morning chill, Kathy hurried from the lobby to the car. In one hand she carried a manila folder.

"This is your present from Rebecca Wylie."

"Just in time. Thanks."

She tugged at the hem of her skirt. "What's going on?"

I stepped on the accelerator and filled her in.

She pulled the collar of her car coat tighter. "So, the two of us are on our way to Plaquemine to kidnap Scot?"

"As a legal technicality, exactly." I slipped between two sixteen wheelers climbing slowly up the ramp. "I like to think of it as a rescue."

She laughed. "It's going to be an exciting day." She stretched her legs, relaxed, gazed down at the river. "What part did you have in mind for me?"

"You play yourself. When Mrs. Sonnier comes to the door, tell her you're a reporter from *The Advocate* and have come to interview her. While she's busy with you, I'll go round back and hope there's a door open. When I've found him, we get him to the car and get out of there. Her husband's not home, so I don't see how she can stop us."

I moved the Mustang into the passing lane and checked the time. Even if some trouble developed, we could make it. We needed to be back at the courthouse by nine o'clock. "It's not much of a plan. What would you do?"

She held up me her cellphone. "Lon Hinkle. He'll be glad to help."

"You think he can?"

"His radio show comes on at six… he's already on air. I'll ask him to broadcast a plea for help. Hundreds of people donated to the Connor Fund and remember the ladies on the steps of the courthouse with their 'Free Connor' signs? Some of them will come." She dialed. "Hi, Lon, this is Kathy. I'm with Jack. We're headed for a Mrs. Sonnier's house in Plaquemine. We're trying to bring Scot to court to testify at nine this morning. He's been hidden away with a cousin. We could use some help. The Sonniers' is just past the bayou—third road to the left after the bridge. Thanks."

She hung up. "He'll get my message. He'll do something. I'm in need of coffee, Jack."

"Okay—and anyway we need to give Lon time to send help. There's a Quik Pak at the bottom of the bridge."

From the middle of the bridge, the view below was splendid. The great ocean ships shone out in the dark, their lights shimmering on the water. Seeing such grand ships, filled with Cargill grain enough to feed the world, was a window into the world of commerce. But this morning they seemed small and unimportant.

We left the Quik Pak, coffee and donuts in hand, and drove beside broad fields planted with soy beans. The little town of Plaquemine lay just behind a canal bridge where the road tightened in a sharp curve. Once past the curve, the highway straightened and ran due south to the Gulf.

Kathy turned from the window. "How much farther?"

"We're almost there."

"I hope you're right about Mrs. Sonnier being alone."

This was no time to worry. The morning could go terribly wrong. Even now some quirk of fate could interrupt my dream of living in Florida, reduce my plan to a passing fancy. I stole a quick glance at Kathy. She was an adventurer, not bound by convention. Was it wishful thinking to ask her to say good-by to Baton Rouge? What might become of us if we left the world behind, drove straight through to the Gulf and Grand Isle? We could install ourselves in a cabin and exchange vows never to return to the mainland. How long could we ignore the attractions of the world? How many years would pass before the loss became too great and one of us broke under the strain of the simple life and returned to civilization?

Kathy said, "We're almost there."

We had reached the bayou. I turned onto the third dirt road and drove on. Two miles later Mrs. Sonnier's house was on the left. The place was in darkness except for one light on in the rear of the house.

"Looks like she's awake," Kathy said.

"Drinking her morning coffee? Stay here while I look around."

At the back of the house, I peered into the window. There she was, a woman with short dark hair wearing a white cotton shirt and lavender panties. I hurried back to the car.

"She's in the kitchen, half-dressed."

"Great. We're in luck."

"Let's get started. You talk first—you're a woman, she won't be frightened of you."

On the porch, we rang the bell, heads bowed. The buzzer sounded but there was no response. I pressed the bell again, and the door opened. Before me stood Mrs. Sonnier.

I was taken aback at the sight of her face to face. From the window I had only seen the back of her, noted the lavender panties, and completely missed the size of her breasts. Large with nipples pointed at me through her T-shirt, they were hard to ignore.

She took her time looking us over. She was not going to be a woman easily unnerved. "You two want something?"

Thrown off balance by the sight of her, I blurted out, "We've come for Scot."

Her eyes narrowed. "Just who the hell are you, Mister?"

I nodded back in respect to her question. "This is Kathy, a reporter for *The Morning Advocate*. I'm an attorney."

She gave us a hard look. "I've got no truck with newspaper people. Got no use for you either, Mister. I know who you are. You're the lawyer helping Connor."

Kathy spoke up. "Mrs. Sonnier, you're guilty of obstructing justice by hiding Scot. That's a crime." That wasn't exactly true, but I liked the tone of it.

Mrs. Sonnier began yelling and pointing. "I want you off my land! I've had enough of the both of you."

It was time to worry. Folks who lived around Plaquemine took property rights to heart. When any of them ordered you off their land, it meant they had a shotgun within easy reach.

Kathy's voice was cool as the morning air. "Are you threatening us, Mrs. Sonnier? Because you're just adding to your problems if you are."

"Shit, lady, you're dumb as a post. I'm fixin' to shoot you."

"Very well, we'll leave." I pulled at Kathy.

She gave me a look but allowed me to lead her away from the porch. As we reached the car she whispered, "We're not really leaving, are we?"

"No, I'm going back. You stay in the car. When I'm halfway to the porch start honking the horn and don't stop."

"Honk the horn?" She grimaced in disbelief.

"It'll wake Scot. He'll look out and see the Mustang and realize I've come for him. Trust me. It'll work."

Mrs. Sonnier was still in the doorway watching us as I turned back toward the house. "You forget something?"

I stalled for time, walked slowly toward her. "I'd like you to reconsider."

The horn blared. It was loud, but I wished it were louder. In the heavy morning air the sound might not carry enough to wake Scot.

"Mister, you're crazy as a loon. Tell your friend to stop her honking or I'll shoot."

"The horn is stuck. She can't help it."

"Stuck my ass! You're trying to wake the boy."

She slipped back into the house. Instinct took over and I ran for the door, but I was too late. She slammed it before I reached the top step. Kathy's honking continued.

I yelled, "Scot, it's me—Jack! Make a run for it!"

Suddenly the door swung open. A shotgun pointed at my chest. "I've had enough, Mister…I'm gonna shoot."

"But there's no reason." I tried to remain calm.

She began swinging the shotgun, moving it back and forth. "I want you off my land."

Once she ordered me off her land, I had no right to be there. I was an attorney, an officer of the court, committing criminal trespass. I could be disciplined for such, even disbarred.

"Okay, I'm leaving."

"Stop talking and get moving." She took a step toward me.

The first sign something was happening was the way Mrs. Sonnier let the gun drop to her side. She rushed past me down the steps. "Come back here, Scot! You come back here!"

I watched as she broke in an all-out run, her legs covering the ground with a female motion, her lavender panties in full view. Searching the yard, I spotted Scot going at a good clip himself and, with his head start, he would reach the Mustang first. Kathy opened the door and Scot jumped in to safety.

Mrs. Sonnier stood beside the car, her breasts heaving. "Come out of that car, Scot Padget. Come out right this minute."

Kathy was still honking when Mrs. Sonnier moved back several paces from the car and wheeled toward me. "That boy's not leaving here. Not as long as I have this shotgun." She raised the gun and pulled the trigger, blowing the Mustang's front tire to shreds.

The pellets made black specks as they ripped through the front fender. The tire was destroyed. Kathy, Scot, and I were going nowhere.

From the direction of the river came a deep-throated chug-a-chug sound, and I located a large dot in the morning sky. The sound grew louder as it neared. The Channel Nine helicopter's orange and white striping swirled as it swept upward in an arc and landed thirty yards away. The door opened and Joe Reed leaped out, his cameraman beside him.

He pulled up beside me. "Where's the boy?"

"He's fine. He's in the Mustang."

Reed went to the car and bent down to peer in. His arm shot up into the air as a signal. "Bring the camera, Bruce. The boy's here all right." The cameraman zipped past me, was halfway to the car when Reed caught sight of Mrs. Sonnier. "Who's the lady?" he yelled over the noise.

"Mrs. Sonnier. This is her house."

He edged around the rear of the Mustang for a better view. "My God, a woman in lavender panties with a shotgun. This is great!"

Mrs. Sonnier reacted in a voice cold with anger. "Mister, get that machine off my land."

Reed began to circle. "Hurry, Bruce. Wonder of wonders." His cameraman beside him now, he stopped circling Mrs. Sonnier and made his way toward the car and Kathy. "For Christ's sake, look at this tire!" He turned toward me. "Damn, Jack, this lady shotgunned your car. You were in serious trouble. I've always said listening to Lon Hinkle pays off."

Mrs. Sonnier seemed stunned for the moment. The cameraman was busy videotaping, and I stood watching the two newsmen go about their business. Then I caught sight of dust rising along the dirt road and a line of cars.

"It's a damn parade!" Reed shouted. "The power of communication. Good God, this is great!"

Through the dust they came, honking their horns. The lead SUV pulled to a stop, and a lady dressed in jeans, her blond hair in a ponytail, stepped out. I thought she looked familiar but couldn't be sure. She pulled a Save Connor sign from the SUV, and I recognized her as one of the supporters from the courthouse steps. Other ladies joined her, holding up their own handmade placards. The clamor of voices grew.

A shotgun blast rent the air. Mrs. Sonnier stood out in the open for all to see. "That's a warning…get off my land!" She lifted her gun toward the women.

The ponytailed leader stood her ground. "You're on TV, Mrs. Sonnier, and as good as naked." She pointed toward the cameraman.

Bruce wheeled into position and beckoned for Mrs. Sonnier to come closer. "Hold it right there…"

She looked at Bruce, suddenly froze in place, then turned and ran for the house.

The blonde extended her hand. "Alma Palmer. Glad we got here in time."

I pointed to the Mustang's tire. "Can we ride with you?"

Joe Reed grabbed my arm. "Come with us in the helicopter. It's quicker."

Ms. Palmer stepped closer to the car. "We can fix this… you just get out of here."

I turned to catch up with Kathy and Scot. Bruce backed towards us, still taking shots of the scene. As soon as he jumped in, the pilot lifted off from the ground.

***

Connor was furious. "Christ, Jack, I told you. Scot is not going to take the stand." His face was red.

"Settle down, Connor." I was pleased at what I had accomplished but not surprised at his outburst. "Scot's here, and he's going to take the stand. You can't change that. You'll only upset him if you don't calm yourself down."

"You're fired, Jack. I'll get another lawyer."

"If you like. But you have to ask Judge LeBlanc, and he won't agree. Not with the case ready to go to the jury, and not on the grounds that you object to a witness whose testimony is going to help you."

"I want to see the judge."

Lieutenant Trahan and the other deputy politely turned away, pretending they could ignore us. The clock on the wall showed eighteen minutes before the trial was to resume. Not a particularly good time to bring an irate client to the judge, but that was the situation I'd gotten myself into. "I'll ask Judge LeBlanc to see you."

I went into the courtroom, which was already filling, the reporters lined together in the front row near the jury box. Kathy wasn't with them, which meant she had taken Scot somewhere more private.

I went straight through the door behind the judge's bench and stood looking down at Miss Idell.

She smiled "Good morning. Judge LeBlanc's on the phone, but I'll take him a note. Meanwhile there's coffee if you'd like some." She disappeared, and, when the door reopened, she said, "Yes Jack, he'll see you."

"Morning, Judge. Thank you for allowing me this time."

"Court is ready to begin, Jack."

"I realize that, but my client's requested a meeting with you before the trial resumes."

"Well, I certainly have no desire to meet with him. What on earth does he want—you know I like my trials to start on time."

"He'd like to fire me."

"I must say he's chosen the wrong time for such nonsense."

I remained silent, not wishing to make an apology for Connor.

"Are you in on this, Jack?"

"No, Your Honor, I swear."

"If this is some trick he's thought up to force me to give him a new trial, I'm not going to do it. The state's already spent a great deal of money to try your client, and it's been a fair trial. You agree?'

"I don't have any complaints, sir."

"I think you and Benton have both been doing quite well. But I'll have to speak to this Mr. Padget of yours if that's what he wants."

When I reentered the judge's chambers with Connor, Judge LeBlanc had thought to put on his robe and appeared to have adjusted to granting Connor a hearing. "Mr. Padget, your attorney informs me you wish to relieve him of his duties as your counsel. This trial is almost in the hands of the jury. Therefore, I presume you have serious reasons."

"I don't want my son to testify. Mr. Carney does. That's my reason."

Judge LeBlanc's fingers twiddled in plain view, his eyes resting on the ceiling for a time before he brought them onto Connor. "If I were your attorney, I would put your son on the witness stand just as your attorney wishes to do."

"May I reply, Your Honor?"

"I'll hear you out, but time is not your friend, Mr. Padget."

"Scot isn't your son and he isn't Jack's. He's my son, so what difference is it to you or to Jack? You're a judge and he's a lawyer, and you're only interested in what happens out there in that courtroom. I'm his father. I'm interested in Scot."

"Excuse me, Mr. Padget, if I seemed at first to be overly brief. I sympathize with your reluctance to have your son testify, but I'm afraid this isn't a family decision."

"Your Honor, I'm going to be convicted." Connor hesitated, as if waiting for Judge LeBlanc to agree, but there was only silence. "Anyway, that's how I feel, so what point is there in forcing Scot to testify in public? He's only eleven. It's not worth it."

Judge LeBlanc's finger began to drum against the yellow legal pad on his desk. "Mr. Padget, I recognize you wish to protect your child, but that's not the only issue here. The conduct of this trial—whether you choose to understand or not—is more important than what you may wish. I'm a judge, and it's my duty to see to it that all relevant evidence is presented to this jury so they might make as wise a decision as they're able. Therefore, I believe it would be best for everyone that I order your son to testify as the court's own witness. Do each of you understand?"

Connor didn't answer, merely looked away.

"Jack, do you understand me?

"Yes, Your Honor, the boy's downstairs. I'll go get him."

"Fine."

30

Dressed in a yellow plaid shirt and blue jeans which Kathy had purchased at Walmart, Scot sat in the witness chair.

"How old are you, Scot?" Judge LeBlanc asked.

"Eleven, sir."

"Do you understand what it means to swear an oath to tell the truth?"

"You promise God to tell the truth when you answer a question."

"If you swear an oath to God it means you believe in Him. Do you?"

"Yessir, I go to school at Saint Agnes."

"The court accepts this young man as a witness and rules that he is competent to testify."

Miss Idell came forward, held out a Bible for Scot. "Raise your right hand and place your left hand on the Bible. Do you swear the testimony you will give in this trial will be the truth, the whole truth, and nothing but the truth, so help you God?"

"Yes, ma'am."

Miss Idell returned to her stenotype machine. I walked to the front of the witness box.

"Scot, your father and mother no longer live together, is that correct?"

"Yessir, my father moved out."

"Did that upset you?"

"I worried I wouldn't get to see him."

"You were busy, weren't you? You played basketball, took karate lessons, right?"

"Yessir."

"And you liked your coaches, didn't you?"

"Father Lieux is my basketball coach. He's nice."

"What about your karate teacher, Alfred Pohl?"

"At first he was nice."

"At some point, you and he went to Memphis for a karate tournament, is that correct?"

"Yessir."

"How did you do in your matches?"

"I lost both my matches."

"Was there any particular reason you didn't do well?"

"One of the other coaches said he felt sorry for me. That I shouldn't have been in the tournament. He said it was for advanced students not beginners."

"Did you ask Pohl why he placed you with advanced students?"

"He said he had his reasons, but he didn't like it when I asked him."

"Did you come home when the tournament ended? You were supposed to be finished Saturday night and return Sunday as I understand it."

He shook his head. "No, Mr. Pohl said he had some business to do. He was waiting on some people to come to Memphis. He told me he'd talked to my mother and she'd said it was okay."

"Did you believe him?"

"At first I did. He told me we would go home Monday in the evening. When we didn't, I thought he wasn't telling me the truth."

"Why did you begin to think that, Scot?"

"My mother didn't let me miss school. She was real strict about that."

"Were there any other reasons?"

"I wanted to call Mother, and he wouldn't let me. He said he'd talked to her and that was good enough."

"Did you get upset? Did you complain?"

"Yes sir. That's when he bought me a PlayStation 2 and a video game."

"This was on the Monday after the tournament, is that correct?"

"Yes sir."

"Did Pohl talk on the phone very often while you were at the house?"

"Yessir. He would talk a long time. He would go outside so I couldn't hear. He would say he was talking business with the men that were coming to Memphis."

"Did you ever hear him say anything about money?"

"I heard him mention money once. He said it should be worth fifty thousand dollars."

"Was he outside when you heard that?"

"Yessir. I raised the window in the kitchen. That's when I heard him say it."

"Did you overhear anything else?"

"He said they had to be in Memphis by Thursday. He said he couldn't wait any longer. It would be too risky. He said he'd already taken too many risks."

"Did he sound angry?"

"I guess—but his back was turned. He must have heard me open the window though 'cause he turned around, and when he saw me at the kitchen window, he got mad. He shoved the phone in his pocket and told me, 'Too bad. You probably just lost your chance to get into the movies.'"

"What happened next?"

"I went to my room. That's when I decided to run away. I didn't trust him anymore. He wouldn't let me call home. I knew something was wrong."

"What day was that?"

"That was Monday. In the morning I just waited and stayed out of his way. I ran away that afternoon—he had to go into town for groceries."

"Tell the jury how you managed that."

"The house we stayed in was on a dirt road out in the country. We didn't have any neighbors. So, I walked along that road until I reached a highway."

Scot was doing what I'd asked of him. He looked me in the eye and spoke carefully. He never looked around the courtroom. "What happened when you reached the highway?"

"A man driving a pickup truck stopped for me. He took me to a Quik Pak. That's where I called my mother."

"Your Honor, I ask your indulgence." I withdrew from my briefcase copies of the FBI dossier on Pohl. With the papers in hand I addressed the court. "I have this morning received crucial information the District Attorney is unaware of. As I intend to place this dossier in evidence, I ask the court for a brief conference."

Judge LeBlanc gave a tap with his gavel. "Gentlemen, please approach the bench."

I handed each of them a copy. "This is an official FBI document, properly certified and attested to. It's the criminal background of Allen Barker, whom we know as Alfred Pohl. It shows he was convicted of counterfeiting and had two arrests for kidnapping. No information is given as to why he never stood trial for the kidnapping, but we all know there are many reasons that can happen. What's important is such arrests create a thread that can be pieced together with his other behavior. For instance, he lived in three different cities in California, all within twenty minutes of Los Angeles and closely tied to the movie industry. One in particular, Culver City, is known to be heavily connected to the production of child snuff films. Your Honor, I firmly believe that was his motive in kidnapping Scot."

Judge Leblanc looked at Benton. "What do you say, counselor?"

"Your Honor, the record of the deceased shows only that Pohl was a criminal as to his conviction for counterfeiting. He was never brought to trial on the charge of kidnapping. The obvious reasons this could happen are that the district attorney decided he was innocent or that proving guilt beyond a reasonable doubt was a problem."

Judge LeBlanc turned to me. "Do you have anything to add, Mr. Carney?"

"That I do, Your Honor. My client is on trial for his life. He faces a possible permanent loss of freedom. We shouldn't take that lightly—and thank the Lord we don't. The deceased has a past worth close scrutiny. Not everything in this world has to be proven to be a fact. Some things we have gut feelings about. Sometimes that's how we reach the truth. This dossier establishes a pattern. Any reasonable man can see that. Why not let the jury decide? Is the district attorney afraid of the jury? It's always important that any evidence that supports the defense must be allowed at a trial. To withhold such is against our sense of justice."

Benton took a long look at Connor before he spoke. "I admit the arrests do have some probative value. In view of the seriousness of the charge, I'll make no objection to the document. The jury can make of it what they will."

Judge Leblanc gave a quick tap with his gavel. "It is ordered that this document be admitted as evidence and marked as defendant exhibit five." He looked to the jury. "Ladies and Gentlemen, this FBI document outlines the criminal background of Alfred Pohl. Copies will be made available to you. Note that the name Alfred Pohl was an alias, that the true name of the deceased was Allen Barker. To avoid confusion, the court will continue to refer to the deceased as Alfred Pohl. Now, as to the document, you may consider this information indicative of what Mr. Pohl was up to in Memphis."

The judge turned to me. "Do you have any further questions?"

"No, Your Honor."

"The district attorney may cross-examine the witness."

"The state has no questions."

Judge LeBlanc looked at Scot. "You may step down, son. You're a fine young man." He turned to me. "Mr. Carney, do you have any further witnesses?"

I didn't answer at once. I was watching Scot. His shoulders were firmly set, his eyes looking straight ahead. Suddenly he smiled. I looked to the gallery and saw Father Lieux. He gave Scot a quick thumbs up as he passed. Alma was sitting next to him.

"Your Honor, the defense rests."

The Judge turned his attention to Benton. "Does the district attorney have any witnesses in rebuttal?"

"The state has none. The state rests its case."

Judge LeBlanc tapped his gavel three times. "The court will allow thirty minutes before closing statements if counsels wish."

Benton hunched his shoulders. "The state is prepared to argue immediately, Your Honor."

"And you, Mr. Carney?"

"The defense is ready, Your Honor."

The judge nodded to the district attorney. "You may proceed."

Benton walked to the far corner of the jury box. He lingered there, then slowly retraced his steps, studying the jurors as he moved. "The State of Louisiana has charged Connor Padget with the crime of murder in the second degree, which is punishable by a sentence of life in prison. To prove the defendant guilty, the state need only show that he acted with a specific intent to kill or inflict great bodily harm when he shot Alfred Pohl."

Benton raised his voice and continued to move about. "How clear can it be? You've seen the television tape. You've witnessed the crime as it was being committed. You've seen Alfred Pohl bound in handcuffs, unable to defend himself, shot down by the defendant. Ladies and gentlemen, you were witness to an execution."

Benton gestured toward me, lowering his voice. "Jack Carney is doing what he can to distract you from the truth. He would have you view Mr. Padget's act of murder as somehow justified." Benton paused and opened his jacket and gazed at Connor. "What is society to do with a man like Connor Padget? A man who has gotten things so terribly wrong. Mr. Padget does not come before you to seek justice, for he is guilty. On the contrary he asks for sympathy." He turned away from Connor to look at the jury. "As jurors you swore no oath to sympathy. Your oath was to justice. Ultimately, it's the law which binds us together as a society. We either seek to live in justice under the law, or we seek to live in chaos. If you do your duty, you'll find the defendant guilty. I wish to thank you for your service as jurors, which has taken you away from your work and your families. Thank you all."

When Benton was seated, I walked toward the jury box carrying in my hand a six-week-old copy of *The Morning Advocate*. "Ladies and Gentlemen, I too want to thank you for your time. I also wish to tell you a story. It is the story of what occurred right here in Baton Rouge some weeks ago." I folded *The Advocate* in half, showed both halves to the jury. "The story I am referring to did not appear on the front page of *The Advocate*. It was buried on page thirteen. Why the *Advocate* paid so little attention to it, I can't say. I do know it's a story worth the telling.

"Near where I live is a Quik Pak convenience store. In the evening, a young lady worked there to support herself and her child. Six weeks ago, I stopped by on my way home from work. I came upon two police cars, their red and blue lights flashing through the darkness. A body lay face down at the front door, glass shattered everywhere. I wondered if it was Nancy.

"An ambulance arrived, and the paramedics lifted the body onto a stretcher. I was relieved to see it was the body of a man.

Peering through the shattered glass, I saw Nancy was safe, standing near the coffee machine talking to one of the police officers. Satisfied she was uninjured, I drove away, turning over in my mind what I had witnessed.

"The following morning, I searched *The Advocate* for news of what I'd seen. On page thirteen, the paper merely noted a man had been killed while attempting to rob a local convenience store. After work, I stopped at the Quik Pak and spoke to a male clerk whom I'd never seen before. When I asked what happened to Nancy, he told me the rest of the story.

"Nancy had given the thief the store's money, then taken the handgun beneath the cash register and shot the thief as he was leaving. She shot him through the glass door. 'What a brave thing to do,' I said to the clerk, for if she had missed, the thief would have turned back and confronted her with his pistol. I asked when she might return to work, and the clerk gave me an odd look and said, 'She works in a new location. That's all I'm allowed to say.'

"It was clear to me that the people who operate these Quik Paks have experience in such matters. They believed Nancy was no longer safe, that the dead man might have friends who would come looking for her."

I glanced at Judy Bradford and saw the look of interest. "Why had she not let the thief just leave? He had reached the door and was on the other side. Why not let him be gone? I tried to think as she must have. Night after night she worked in that store alone, without protection. No doubt at times she felt afraid and helpless. That night I think she'd had enough."

I moved toward Reverend Johnston and looked straight at his face. "Now let us turn to the story of Connor. It's not unlike

Nancy's story. Pohl was like a thief who appeared suddenly, charming Mary Beth and befriending Scot. He was a stranger fishing in troubled waters.

"Convinced his wife had become attracted to this stranger, Connor reacted peacefully. He moved from the home, taking with him the hope that his wife's flirtation would end. And yet Connor's troubles were not at an end, for Pohl was not yet through with him. Now a mentor of Scot, Pohl brought the boy to Memphis and hid him away from the family. Take a moment, if you will, to imagine what must have been going through Connor's mind. In some way he had failed his wife, and his marriage was in trouble, and now he had failed to protect his son. Do any of you doubt he felt threatened? Like Nancy at the Quik Pak, he reached the point where enough was enough, and he reacted."

I glanced towards the judge. "Judge LeBlanc will instruct you as to the law which you are to follow in reaching your decision. One such instruction will deal with the crime of manslaughter. Briefly stated it is this: manslaughter is a homicide committed in sudden passion immediately caused by provocation sufficient to deprive the average person of self-control or cool reflection."

I gestured toward Connor. "The jurisprudence in Louisiana is on the side of the defendant." Pausing, I searched for Reverend Johnston. "The courts of this state have held that an act of adultery is sufficient provocation to justify a jury returning a verdict of manslaughter rather than murder when one spouse has been charged with the killing of the other. Connor suffered much more: the kidnapping of his son to be sold as chattel."

I folded *The Advocate* three times and struck it against the palm of my hand. "There exists today a corruption in our society which passes all understanding. It is the human trafficking of our children who are stolen away from their families to be sold, to be used as sex slaves, or murdered in snuff films. We can never be certain which purpose Pohl had in mind for Scot, but we do know he had plans.

"We also know Pohl had been twice arrested for child kidnapping. We know these arrests took place while he was living in California in an area given over to the making of films. We know he was into criminal activity, and through aliases and falsified documents, managed to evade the law. We know he was hiding Scot in Memphis, waiting. Waiting for what? Surely, he was waiting for his money, his fifty thousand dollars. Surely, he was waiting for the people he was dealing with to come for Scot.

"Do you have before you absolute proof of what Pohl was up to? No, you do not. But what you do have is sufficient evidence to form a reasonable belief and under the law that is enough."

I turned toward Connor. "The defendant is a decent man and, much like Nancy, someone caught up in circumstances not of his own making. Connor killed someone and so did Nancy, but neither are criminals." I lowered my voice. "Every day as you come to this courtroom you've seen the women on the courthouse steps with their placards. Their presence pleads with you not to take Scot's father from him. Not to brand Scot's father as a criminal, for he knows he is not one. The shooting of Pohl took place in public. The district attorney was forced to bring charges against Mr. Padget. Sometimes I believe his heart wasn't in it. Separating a young boy from his father is a terrible thing—I don't believe your heart will be in it either.

"Thank you."

***

Seated beside Connor in the holding room, I was drained. I could no longer remember simple matters. I wasn't hungry but could not be certain I had eaten. Connor and I had not spoken since we entered the room to wait. At some point, it occurred to me that the time would pass easier if we talked.

"Could I bring you a coffee?"

"No thanks, Jack." He shifted in his chair. "I didn't see Mary Beth when I looked for Scot."

"She violated the subpoena for him to testify. She's subject to arrest. I would've stayed away myself."

"I'd like to see him. Is that possible?"

"I'll go look."

Happy to have something to tend to, I opened the holding room door. The two deputies standing guard let me pass. Kathy would probably be in an empty courtroom, and Scot would be with her. I made my way to the corridor and opened each door carefully, listening for the sound of lawyers at work. In Judge Hunter's courtroom I found all three of them: Scot, Kathy, and Rebecca Wylie. Ms. Wylie spoke first. "I'm having a word with Scot. I hope you don't mind."

I looked at Ms. Wylie, thought how there was a time I might have resented her using the boy to satisfy her readers' curiosity, but that time had passed. She was a fair-minded woman who had been of great help. She was a journalist doing what journalists do, just as I was an attorney doing what attorneys do.

"Connor would like to visit with Scot," I said. Scot scooted from his chair, the new tennis shoes Kathy had bought him flashing as he ran.

I was closing the courtroom door when Ms. Wylie spoke up again, "Don't forget our interview, Jack."

"I'll call you tomorrow."

"Call me, too!" Kathy waved goodbye.

I waved back. "I'll check in with the both of you."

For the next two hours, I sat with Connor and Scot, watching them eat Fig Newtons and drink Pepsi Colas. When the watching and waiting became too much, I went for a walk through the corridors of the courthouse. Many lawyers clung to the adage that jury verdicts were unpredictable, but deep down I thought to say such was something of a pretense. "You can never tell what a jury will do" is what lawyers say in public, as though a jury verdict was nothing more than a ball cast onto a roulette wheel. I'd done a decent job. I had gotten across the difference between murder and manslaughter. Surely in the end, the jury would see Connor as I did.

In my wanderings in the hallway, I happened upon Judge Hardin's courtroom. Not ready to return to the holding room, I opened the door and went in. Judge Hardin gave me a nod, and I chose a seat in the back row. A nurse was explaining the hospital's procedures to minimize the risk of a wrong limb being taken. If I were to give up being a lawyer, I would miss the drama. And yet, if I actually moved to Florida, I didn't doubt I would be content sailing the Gulf waters with tourists come down from the North to vacation. The future was like that. It was full of possibilities while bits and pieces of the past stayed with you.

The nurse's voice began to fade. Sloan and I were standing shoulder to shoulder on the stage of a Tokyo cabaret singing, "You are lost and gone forever, oh my darling, Clementine." We were in the Shinjuku district, a place where no Americans or Europeans ventured, and we were having the time of our lives. Over the glare of the floodlights you could see the faces of the

Japanese. They were no longer passive and inscrutable. They were clapping, whistling, and cheering. They had come to be entertained, and we were their fun.

The manager, wearing a dark suit, came toward us bearing two quart bottles of Ashi beer. He bowed when he presented them, which set off another round of cheering and clapping. As I bowed, I caught sight of Yoko, the girl Sloan intended to marry, a waitress at Yokota's Officer Club. She liked Sloan, and he spoke her language fluently. Now in a shy Japanese way she lifted her hand to her face to hide her giggling.

Beside me Sloan asked, "Can you sing "I've Been Working on the Railroad?" He didn't wait for my answer and started in on his own. I knew the words well. The manager suddenly appeared, holding another quart bottle in each hand. "He always likes me to sing three songs," Sloan whispered.

"You've done this before."

"He likes Yoko, so he likes me."

This time we were ready when Nobuaki bowed before handing us the beer. We all bowed as one and the crowd cheered and whistled. In my life I'd never experienced such approval. Sloan knew what to do. He lifted the beers, one in each hand, to salute the audience, and the noise rose again. Caught up in the spirit of the good time, I asked, "Do you know the words to "You are my Sunshine?"

He grinned. "Let's have a go at it, shall we?" And for one last time we started singing. The applause of the crowd, mixed with the lyrics, was the only sound, until a bang of Judge Hardin's gavel interrupted. "This court will stand adjourned until tomorrow at nine-thirty a.m."

I waited for the judge to gather his robes about him and disappear before I left my seat and returned to worrying about Connor. My appetite was coming back, and I decided to settle for a Fig Newton and a bottle of Pepsi.

Soon, I was sitting again with Connor. He brought up the subject of my sailing to Florida. "The rest will do you a world of good, Jack. I hope you'll keep in touch with Scot."

"Sure. I miss flying. Sometimes I wonder if I should join the reserves and do some."

The door opened, and a deputy looked in. "Jury's back."

Connor looked at me. "What do you think? Good or bad?"

I lifted my palms in a gesture of hope. "No one knows what a jury will do. Just always pray for the best."

Inside the courtroom Benton sat at his counsel table, looking neither left nor right. Scot sat between Kathy and Ms. Wylie on the back row. I watched the jurors carefully as they filed in one after the other. Their faces were blank, devoid of emotion, and though I had little reason to be hopeful, I was.

Once the jury took their seats Judge LeBlanc wasted no time. "Ladies and gentlemen, have you reached a verdict?"

Reverend Johnston stood. "We have, Your Honor."

Judge LeBlanc spoke in a sober voice, "Thank you, Mr. Foreman. The clerk will collect the verdict."

Miss Idell rose from her desk, took the paper, and handed it to the judge. Judge LeBlanc unfolded the note, read it, and returned it to Miss Idell. "The defendant will rise, and the foreman will read the verdict."

The foreman read quickly. "We, the members of the jury, find the defendant, Connor Padget, guilty of the crime of manslaughter."

The courtroom became a place of sounds. The spectators fell to murmuring, and a rustling arose of people shifting and moving in their seats. Beside me Connor was calm, his face set. I leaned toward him, said what I knew to be true. "It's the best we could hope for."

He answered quietly, as a man at peace with himself might do. "You did great, Jack."

I glanced behind me. Scot wasn't crying and didn't appear to be on the verge of tears. He had the look of a child waiting for someone to explain what had happened. Earlier, before the reading of the verdict, two deputies had positioned themselves behind Connor and me. Soon they would walk him from the courtroom into the elevator that led to the jail, and Connor's new way of living would begin.

Judge LeBlanc allowed a brief interval to pass before he spoke. "Will the defendant and the attorneys please rise." We did. "The court is prepared to impose sentence. If the defendant wishes a delay, the court will grant it."

I turned to Connor. "Do you prefer to wait?"

"Let's be done with it."

"Your Honor, my client waives his right to delay."

Judge LeBlanc wasted no time. "Connor Padget, you have been found guilty of the crime of manslaughter. The maximum sentence for such a crime is forty years in prison at the State Penitentiary at Angola. Considering the evidence presented during trial, the court is of the opinion that you are not a threat to society and is inclined to show leniency. Therefore, it is the sentence of this court that you serve ten years at the State Penitentiary and shall be eligible for parole upon serving one third of the sentence."

Connor turned to me, looking neither grim nor happy. "I thank God for what you did for me, Jack. I'll see my boy again."

I smiled. "Yes, you will, Connor, and he'll only be fourteen when you return home."

The deputies took Connor by the arms, gently walking him away, then stopped when they saw Scot and Kathy waiting for them to pass. Connor bent to kiss Scot on the cheek. "Don't worry. I'll be fine." The moment was over. The deputies led him toward the door that led to the elevator that would take him to the jail.

I made my way down the stairs, glad to feel the outside again. The sun was shining. When I reached the car and opened the door, I was surprised to see Adrienne.

"I've been waiting for you," she said. "You were wonderful, and I wanted you to know I'm proud of you."

"I didn't think you'd come. But it means a lot to me."

"What are you going to do now?" she asked.

Without hesitation I said, "Just think it all over...and go sailing."

"Will you keep in touch now and then?"

"I will. Perhaps life will give us a second chance."

She gave me her best smile. I watched as she walked away to see if she would look back. She didn't.

31

Standing on the veranda of the Mandeville Yacht Club, Ted Scullen, Miles Favrot, and I gazed at the waters of Lake Pontchartrain. The Louisiana Supreme Court had declared it to be "an arm of the sea" since it led to the waters of the Gulf of Mexico. It was for me a pathway to Florida. Farewells signify, for they have meaning, and today I was wearing the black bowler hat I had worn so proudly to our squadron parties in Japan.

Miles sipped his rum and coke. "You're really leaving us?"

Of the three of us, he was the best sailor. He took a sabbatical from the New Orleans law firm of Harrison & Boyd to sail solo to Martinique and Saint Kitts, and it was he who suggested we drink rum, the drink of sailors, to memorialize my going.

Scully answered for me. "I helped Jack stock the Yarnspinner. Lots of canned goods, dried fruit, and ice. He's going, all right."

"And I thank you for your help, Scully." These two were the perfect ones to see me off. Neither had made any mention of Connor's trial, and for that I was grateful.

"I declare," said Miles, "we're in need of another rum."

Scully emptied what was left in his glass in a single swallow. "Let's fetch another."

"Right you are. Drinks all around." The two went off, and I was left alone with time to think. The sun was still visible but moving faster now as it neared the horizon. I turned away from the lake, looked through the glass windows of the clubhouse, and studied the two of them standing at the bar. Both were older, had already lost their wives along the way. They practiced law in a fashionable way in the better part of New Orleans and had homes on the fairways of the Covington Country Club. On Saturdays they sailed in the Gulf, then spent the evening in the Club's grill room playing poker and drinking gin and tonics. Perhaps one day I might return to live such a life myself. It was something to keep in mind as a possibility if Florida wasn't the answer.

My thoughts drifted, taking me back to Yokota and the day of my leaving Japan. I was walking again beneath the ornate oriental archway with a tear in my eye. The control tower piped the song Sayonara onto the runway as I climbed into an Air Force C-130. I was alive. I was going home, far away from this foreign land. I could barely grasp the truth of it all, for not everyone in my squadron had been so lucky.

On the last evening, the squadron had celebrated my good fortune. As was our tradition, we dressed in our Class-A uniforms, wore our British bowler hats, and marched through each room of the Officers Club, receiving nods and smiles from those we passed. Our march ended outside on the bricked patio where we stood in a chilly soft winter rain, but no one complained. Each of us had learned that the coming and goings of life could not be postponed, and we took the weather as it was.

Sounds of footsteps cut short my looking back. I turned to see Miles and Scully walking towards me, drinks in hand. Scully held out a rum drink. "Should old acquaintance be forgot."

Miles, with his engineer's blood, was disinclined to moments of hearts and flowers. "Jack's just on sabbatical. He'll come sailing home to us one day."

I sipped at the rum and coke. The bartender had added a slice of orange; it cheered me he knew who the drink was for. "Listen up," I said. "I'll teach you an Air Force good-bye."

"Does it include a toast?" asked Miles.

"More than one." I held out my bowler. "First we pour our drinks into the hat. Then we pass it around—three times—we all know things come in threes. After a second round, the man being toasted steps into the middle of the circle to dance a jig. The passing begins again until the man who drinks last throws his glass at the feet of the dancing man. This is the signal for the rest of the men to throw theirs."

"That's a lot of broken glass," said Miles. "We'll need more drinks to do the bowler justice."

"I'll fetch reinforcements." Scully set off for the Grill Room. In no time he returned pushing a serving cart with empty glasses and a half-filled bottle of rum. "Now we're in business." He reached for my bowler and poured in the rum.

The passing of the hat began. With two rounds complete, I stepped forward between the two of them and began my jig, hopping and turning in grand style. Nods of approval egged me on, and their turns at the draught were taken with extra cheers. It was not long before Scully let forth a holler, declaring the last drop had been drunk. He hurled his glass. It was a good throw and shattered at my feet. Miles added his with a shout, "Hooray for the Yokota good-bye!" The glass shattered at my feet with great panache. The three of us fell into laughing and hugging.

We were still enjoying ourselves when, looking down from the veranda, we watched a Dixie Cab pull to a stop. "Someone's obviously lost," Miles said. "I'll go see if they need directions."

He had barely reached the steps when out popped Scot Padget, looking up at us and waving. "It's me, Mr. Carney."

Afraid that some misfortune had brought the boy to Covington, I swung over the railing, dropped to the ground, and grasped him by the shoulders. "Has something happened?"

He was happy and smiling. "Nothing's wrong. I'm fine."

The driver of the Dixie Cab leaned his head through the window. "If the boy's going to be okay, I'll be leaving."

"What do we owe you for the fare?" I asked.

"He's a nice kid. Take care of him." He drove away. The lettering on the side of the car read Dixie Cab, Covington, Louisiana.

"How did you get from Baton Rouge to Covington?"

"I have money. I bought a ticket at the bus station in Baton Rouge, then I took a taxi here from Covington. He didn't even charge me." He was proud of himself.

I was still trying to sort things out. "You're an independent kid, I'll give you that." I led him up to the veranda. "Gentlemen, this is Scot, the son of Connor Padget. Scot, this is Ken Scullin and Miles Favrot."

Scot, appearing quite pleased with himself, shook their hands. "Hello, I'm glad to meet you."

Favrot and Scully politely returned the honors, then simply nodded and excused themselves. Waving good-bye, they disappeared back into the Grill Room.

I looked at Scot. "I'm happy to see you, son, but what's going on?"

"I want to go with you to Florida."

"Does your mother know where you are?"

"She thinks I'm at Cortana Mall. I go there on Saturdays with my friends."

"We need to call her."

His smile disappeared, and he stepped away from me. "I'm not going back. You can't make me."

This was a delicate moment and it would be wise to take care. I was dealing with a troubled boy, not some parcel delivered to a wrong address to be bundled up and shipped back.

"Even if you came with me to Florida, you couldn't stay. You'd have to go back at some point, Scot."

"Dad said you'd take care of me."

"I'm sorry, Scot. I'm on my way to Sanibel. You barely caught me."

"I want to go with you, Mr. Carney. That's why I'm here."

"Your mother won't like this. Does she know where you are?"

"No."

"We need to call her."

"I won't be any trouble."

"If you go to Florida, you won't be able to visit Connor. Now Mary Beth will take you…just like I took you to the jail."

"It's not the same. I thought he was coming home when I went with you."

"I'm going to the other end of the porch. I need to talk to Mary Beth. You stay here, okay?" I pulled out my cell. She answered before I was halfway.

"I recognized your number, Jack. I thought you'd be gone by now."

"We have a problem. "I'm at the yacht club in Mandeville. I'm trying to leave for Sanibel. Scot showed up and wants to go with me to Florida. Did you realize he was that unhappy?"

"Good Lord, Jack!" She was silent. I heard her put the phone down and her footsteps as she walked away. I waited. Finally, she was back. Her voiced seemed calmer. "Jack, how did he even get down there? I dropped him off at the mall. He likes to go there on Saturdays to play the arcade games with his friends. This is a shock."

"He used his arcade money for a bus ticket. Walked to the Greyhound bus station and got a ticket to Covington, then caught a taxi here. I was saying goodbye to friends when he showed up."

She spoke in a softer voice. "It's true he's been unusually quiet. But I thought that was normal after what's happened. I'm having problems myself, but I should have noticed."

"Don't be mad at him."

"I'm a mother, Jack. No, I'm not mad. I just don't know how to react. It's all been too much for him."

"We need to focus on what's best for Scot. As for me, I'm not sure how long I'll be in Sanibel. I might stay… and I might not."

"What does that have to do with Scot?"

"Maybe he's right. Maybe he should come with me. The trip itself is just three days. He'll love being on a sailboat, and that's good enough for now. When we get there, I can send him back home on a plane. Or I can postpone my going, if you want, and bring him back right now."

"I'm afraid he's trying to run away, Jack. He might want to stay. He might think he can stay there with you if I say yes."

"Well…" I paused. "What if you came down too? It's beautiful there…you might like it."

She hesitated. "Give me some time. I need to think."

I turned to look at the water. The wind was coming up.

When she came back, her voice was steady. "What about the Connor Fund… can I use that? I'd be more willing to say yes if money isn't a problem."

"The money in the fund is for your family. It's yours now."

"Then…that's it. I'll take the chance…let me talk to Scot."

I held the phone high and walked toward Scot. "She said yes…but she wants to talk to you!"

***

The clanking of the halyards striking the masts of the sailboats grew louder. The wind was coming up. Scot and I made our way toward the door to the Club Grill, and I waved for Scully and Favrot to come outside.

"It's time," I said.

Scully grabbed my shoulder. "May the wind be always at your back, and the road rise to meet your feet. Oh…and have fun with the kid, Jack."

"I will. This is something I surely didn't expect." I looked at my watch. It was a little after five. Scot and I walked onto the oyster shell driveway. The chill in the air made for a nice evening and a fitting touch.

"How big is your boat, Mr. Carney?" He turned to face me and happily skipped backwards.

"Thirty-four feet. It's a solid boat, solid enough to sail across the ocean to Europe if I had a mind to."

"I've never been on a sailboat. What's it like?"

"I have it rigged for solo sailing. It has roller furling and roller reefing and it can turn on a dime." I tousled his hair. "Of course, it's easier to sail with two on board, so you can count on helping. And it has a galley, so we'll have warm food. And it sleeps six, so we have plenty of room."

"Is it dangerous being a sailor?"

"Not if you have respect for the sea and look out for the weather. It's when you run into bad weather that trouble begins. Sailing is a lot like flying, Scot. Those who pay little heed to the weather don't often live to see the next day."

"Do you think a storm might hit us?"

"The weather reports promise us four days of good sailing, but we'll stay close to the coastline in case they're wrong." Reaching the dock, I pointed out the Yarnspinner. "What do you think of her?"

"I think she's beautiful." He grinned. "What can I do?" He was quick to jump aboard and look around.

"Go to the front. Sailors call that the bow. You'll pull on that line on your right to reach the cleat on the pier and undo it. Then rewrap it on the boat to be ready again when we dock later."

"Okay." He moved along the deck, grabbing the mast stays for balance. He was a natural.

"Walk back now towards me. After you undo the stern line, we're off."

I started the engine. As the wind hit us, the boat began moving and I pushed the gearshift forward. We picked up speed, and the water made a slapping sound against the hull. We were well out into the lake when we passed a can buoy, the metal ringing out its sounds as it shifted to and fro in the current. I turned the Yarnspinner, headed her south by southeast toward Biloxi.

Scot stared back at the bell marker. "What's a scarecrow doing so far out in the lake?"

"Sailors use them for navigation, but they have other uses as well. Come daylight you'll see seagulls flying in to rest on them."

"That's neat."

"You'll love the night, Scot. Out here, away from the lights of the city, you'll see the stars as they were meant to be seen. They'll be hanging in a sky so black you'll feel like you're the only person in the world."

"I'm going to stay awake all night. I don't want to miss anything."

"We have cokes and root beer below."

"No, thanks. I'll just sit here and watch… Mr. Carney, can I call you Mr. Jack?"

"Sure. I'd like that."

I cut the engine, set the wheel, and unfurled the mainsail. As it rolled out to catch the wind, we tilted to port. I let the genoa go, and we righted and turned back into the wind, which was coming steadily across the boom, pushing us on. If it lasted through the night, by mid-morning we should be off the coast of Biloxi. The two of us were off to a good start.

www.ingramcontent.com/pod-product-compliance
Lightning Source LLC
LaVergne TN
LVHW091537060526
838200LV00036B/648